THE JOURNEYS BEGIN

BEGIN

Ora

E.E. Byrnes

Acknowledgments

I would like to give full recognition and gratitude to Scott Editorial for being the reason this novella exists. From the highest standard of editing to the creative talent in designing the cover, their skilled touch is evident throughout this work.

I would also like to acknowledge my husband, Niall, and dedicate this book to him for his constant support and assistance with researching historical facts.
I am forever grateful to my publishing team and family.

- E.E. Byrnes

First published in Great Britain in 2022 by Book Bubble Press

www.bookbubblepress.com

A CIP record of this book is available from the British Library.
ISBN: 978-1912494-84-2

Chapter One

"The city has been surrendered," Papa said, his voice as grim as his sombre eyes. "General Sherman and his blasted Union Army have finally forced John Bell's hand."

The wooden chair at the dining table scraped across the floor as he sat. The screech it made rattled my nerves and made the hair across my arms rise. The delicious smell of breakfast disappeared, and the warm food in my belly became a cold, hard lump. The Union Army had arrived in July, and our brave soldiers had been trying to fight them off since. But through August, we had watched them grow increasingly tired, the weight of battle and sacrifice of food finally taking its toll on them. I could understand that our Lieutenant General John Bell Hood, who had fought in Antietam and Gettysburg, must have felt he had no choice but to save his dying men.

"We need to leave," Mama said. Her gaze was sharp and focused, but panic lined her eyes, and she took deep, controlled breaths.

My mama was a strong woman. There weren't many things that could make her worry, much less panic. She had survived starvation as a young girl, walked alone on foot through the backwoods of Kentucky with nothing but a cow for company, and travelled to Atlanta, where she found factory work to survive. This desperate childhood had fortified her courage to be the rock she had leaned upon during the past three years of civil war. It had prepared her to deal with hardship, fear, and desperation, which were all factors that this awful war had brought upon us. Until now, I had never heard her warm, mild voice sound panicked.

"This is our home," Papa growled, his teeth clipping his words as he shot a fierce look at her. "I'll be damned if I let those Yanks push us out of it."

His determined words made me glance involuntarily at the three golden stars embroidered on the collar of his grey uniform jacket, along with the sleeve insignia of what looked to be a golden crown. Both identified him as a Confederate Colonel, and Papa wore them with almighty pride. He hadn't reached his high rank due to cowardice. Rebellion lay strong within him, and he wasn't one to retreat from confrontation. Mama laid a gentle hand on Papa's arm, and her soothing touch calmed the flame that ignited his fury.

"The girls, Clarence," she said softly. "We must think of them first. I love our home, but I love our family more."

Papa's nostrils flared with stubborn indignation, but Mama's logic was hard to argue with. He looked over at me as I stared at him, and the hard light in his eyes dimmed to a soft glow. The fight in him deflated, and I watched as his weathered face grew heavy until every age line deepened, making him look ten years older. It made me suddenly realise just how tired the war had made him.

"You're right," he said helplessly. "Our family must come first."

Mama smiled at him gratefully, gave him a light kiss, and then picked up my little sister, Leila, and left the room. Her lips were tight, her eyes were hard, and her face was a frozen mask of determination. Even though my sister was only four years old, she knew better than to protest when Mama was like this. I needed to help Mama. Standing up, I glanced around the elegant dining room, trying to think of a way to help without asking. I'm sixteen years old and old enough to figure out what to do, but panic had slithered its way into my head, freezing all coherent and rational thoughts. I imagined the soldiers breaking down our door, ransacking every room, and arresting Papa, leaving us abandoned and vulnerable to the Union army. These frightening thoughts were interrupted by large fingers tightening on my shoulder, and I looked round as Papa smiled at me.

"Ora, go find your mama," he said, his eyes warm with understanding. "Tell her I'll be getting the carriage ready."

I nodded woodenly as my heart thundered against my chest. I had relied on Mama's strength and wisdom my whole life. Much as she leaned on her rock of courage, I leaned on her. Part of me wanted to prove that I could be like her, while another part knew I still desperately needed her.

"Mama!" I cried out, and my voice rang through the long front hall. I mindlessly exited the dining room and searched the drawing room across from it, fear erasing all logical thoughts about where she

3

might be. I simply searched without thinking, my brain frozen in terror.

My footsteps were soundless on the thick-carpeted floors as I raced down the hall. As I searched the rooms for Mama, my heart squeezed painfully at the realisation that I would never see our house again. At worst, the northerners would burn it to the ground as they raided the city. At best, it would become one of their homes.

"How dare they," I growled, anger fuelling my adrenaline and extinguishing my fear. "These Yankee bastards think they can just march into our city and demand we change our way of life."

Papa had always made decent money as a southern politician. When the war started, he became a Confederate Colonel. Thanks to him, we lived in a nice, comfortable house. It wasn't like the grand plantation homes nestled outside the city amidst their acres of cotton fields, but it had everything one could ask for. Plenty of space, lush furnishings, and solidly built, only for all of it to be taken away. I searched the bedrooms upstairs, but they were empty. My fingers subconsciously gripped my dress as I descended the stairs. Confusion and worry replaced my rage, scattering my thoughts to find answers. Where on earth were Mama and Leila? The house was unnervingly quiet. I didn't see any of the house slaves either, even Phibe, our main slave, who had been with us since I was born. She was usually always near to lend assistance in some way. Mama must have already told them to leave. But why wasn't she around then? My heart started beating so hard that I leaned against a wall to loosen my corset. Logic and emotion went to battle in my head, and I closed my eyes to try to quiet them. Once I stilled

4

my thoughts, I could hear the house around me. The wind blew through the fireplaces, and the wooden walls creaked as they settled. Though it was eerily quiet, I was calm enough to think rationally for the first time. Mama dismissed the slaves. That meant she would have had to go to their quarters.

Although, I reminded myself, *they aren't really our slaves anymore.*

Lincoln had released them a year earlier with his Emancipation Proclamation. Fortunately, Mama and Papa had always been good masters, never whipping in discipline or depriving food. Many of our slaves had stayed with us through loyalty and because they had nowhere else to go. Although Papa could be stricter with them, Mama had always preferred to treat them as hired staff rather than people we owned. We had lost a few due to the Proclamation, but not as many as some households.

I arrived in the empty kitchen. The stairs in there led to the slaves' quarters, but I didn't need to go down them. I instinctively knew there was no one down there. I turned around and saw the open back door that led to the yard. The gentle breeze was swinging it slowly with a soft creak.

"Mama," I whispered.

I charged through the door.

I nearly fell over my heavy skirts as I rushed down the porch steps. I could see Mama at the back of the yard, her dress blowing from the mild summer breeze that fanned the flames of the fires the northerners were setting a few streets from us. Neighbouring rooftops were engulfed, the fires' roars swallowing the distant cries of those who had chosen to rebel. Leila clutched fiercely onto Mama. Her little legs were wrapped tightly around Mama's

5

middle. Tear tracks stained her chubby cheeks, and her eyes were red from crying. Her small knuckles were white as they gripped Mama's dress. Seeing Leila's terror made me want to cry.

"Mama! Sissy!" I cried, clutching Mama's free arm that wasn't holding Leila. I wished for a moment that she could carry me too. "I was so worried."

"Listen," Mama murmured. "You can already hear the screaming."

She was right. Now that I was next to my rock, I settled again, confident that I could face any challenges. Soldiers were evicting anyone who resisted them, and considering the Confederate pride within us, that would be most people. However, Mama was smart. She knew there was no point in resisting.

"Papa told me to tell you that he's getting the carriage ready," I said, happy to finally relay his message.

Mama looked at me. Her deep brown eyes were hard, and her lips were pressed so tight I could hardly see them.

"That's good," she said. "The servants can help him."

Mama had been good about calling them servants once they'd been officially freed. I knew she appreciated the ones who had stayed.

"So you didn't dismiss them?" I asked.

"No," she said mildly, her grip tightening on Leila. "I'm back here because soldiers will be in front of the house if they're nearby. Leila started crying, and I didn't want to attract their attention. They won't be able to hear her from back here."

At the mention of her name, Leila managed to raise her head from Mama's shoulder, her tiny voice so soft we strained to hear it.

"I'll be quiet," she whispered. Her brown eyes were round with fear, but she was calmer now. Her grip had loosened, and her tears had finally dried.

Mama gave a small grin and a brisk nod.

"Alright then," she said firmly. "If you girls can be quiet, we'll go upstairs and grab what clothing we can."

Nothing further was said as we made our way quietly upstairs. I strained to hear any confrontation at the front. Papa would have told the slaves to have the horse and carriage ready for him, so I didn't understand why he had to be with them. The slaves were more than capable.

As we packed what little clothing we could fit into two pieces of luggage, Mama's strained face grew heavier.

"I knew it couldn't last," she muttered suddenly, causing Leila and I to look at her in surprise. "I've had it too good for too long now."

"It'll be fine, Mama," I assured her and tried to sound confident. "It has nothing to do with how good we have it. The northerners just won't understand our way of life."

Mama scoffed a little under her breath and cocked an eyebrow at me. She didn't say anything, but her face softened as she studied me. After a few uncomfortable moments, she spoke, her voice more solemn than I had ever heard before.

"We're going to leave the city for the north. If something happens, take care of your sister."

"Nothing will happen," I argued as fear crept up my chest again.

"I said *if*. We must be prepared for anything."

We picked up the two luggage cases and left the larger trunks we couldn't carry. Leila had to walk behind us, clinging to Mama's dress pleats.

"Must we go north?" I asked. "I can't imagine having to deal with a Yankee personally."

Mama gave a low chuckle before nodding wistfully.

We descended the stairs and stood in our wide front hall. Mama glanced around us at the golden-framed paintings, heavy velvet curtains hanging on the front windows, and the rose-filled porcelain vase sitting on the hall table.

"There's no help for it," she sighed. "It's our best chance for safety. But I will miss our home dearly. I've had a good life in these rooms."

Pearls of tears started to well at the corners of her eyes, but she blinked and took a deep breath. "No use crying over it," she said, her voice quivering. "I've found a new life before, and I can do it again."

Leila and I glanced at each other, both of us worried over how concerned Mama was. We had never seen her nearly in tears before.

"Ora, take your sister's hand. Phibe can carry your other luggage," she ordered firmly. "Where is she?"

I did as she said, and to my relief, so did Leila. I never knew if she would argue or not, but today the fear and chaos around the house had subdued her into obedience.

"I'm right here, ma'am," Phibe said, her wide-hipped frame appearing as if by magic beside us. I wondered briefly where she had been. It was unusual for us to be in the house without Phibe around somewhere. She quickly saw my confused expression at her appearance and smiled warmly. Her caramel eyes welled up as she looked at me.

"I was out helping your papa," she explained hurriedly. "Now, no time to be wastin', girl. We have to get yous all out."

We followed Mama out the front door, leaving a luggage case waiting on the front porch for Phibe to carry behind us. I blinked against the bright sun. The weather was unaware of the day's tragedy. It was humid, hot, and filled with the scent of magnolias. Papa's grey uniform jacket was already soaked with sweat from the dense humidity as he tightened the final strap on the horse's harness.

"We're ready," he said, nearly breathless from anxiety and exertion. "Girls, get into the carriage."

I lifted my skirts, climbed into the back, and turned to lift Leila. We never hesitated when Papa gave a direct order. I watched in subdued silence as Mama and Papa said goodbye to the slaves, standing in a neat row together. They all seemed sombre, and some even looked scared. I could easily imagine why. We were the only home they had ever known. Phibe, Kitch, Tandey, Hany...names of people I had known for most of my life and as familiar to me as my own parents. Phibe particularly since she had helped raise me. Though they were free, they didn't have anywhere to go or anyone to take care of them. I worried for their safety along with ours. I tended to have Papa's habit of still calling them slaves, but I thought of them the same as Mama. They were helpful servants who I respected and couldn't imagine living without. Who would take care of them now?

Chapter Two

Papa climbed up to the driver's seat, and a moment later, the carriage pulled away from the house. As the carriage departed, I watched Phibe burst into tears. Two glistening streams ran down her black cheeks. Whether in happiness that she was free or sadness to see us go, I wasn't sure. Perhaps it was a mixture of both.

"Where will they go?" I asked, leaning forward so Mama could hear me over the rattling of the carriage wheels.

"I'm not sure," she said and shrugged dismissively. "I haven't the slightest notion, but at least we did our part and let them go to try what they will. I expect they'll head north. Maybe even join the Union Army."

With pursed lips and a sharp lift of her shoulder, she said, "I don't even know where exactly we're going yet, though Papa will head toward Cherokee County. As soon as we get safely out of Atlanta, we'll stop at the nearest inn and try to make a more definite plan."

Right before we turned onto the main street, I looked back through the carriage window at our house. It stood like a solid, shining white beacon of comfort. My chest tightened so painfully that tears sprung to my eyes.

"Goodbye, home," I whispered. Mama gave me a sharp look.

"You'll learn to love another," she said firmly, shifting in her seat and holding her head high. "I learned to make Atlanta my home years ago, even though I was born in the Kentucky mountains."

I nodded and wrapped my arm around Leila, who cuddled up against me. Papa was driving slowly to avoid attracting any unnecessary attention. The Union soldiers would be watching for anyone who looked suspicious.

"I travelled for a long time before coming here," Mama continued, her voice pensive and her narrowed eyes combed my face critically. She seemed to be looking for something, but I couldn't imagine what. "I was mainly alone, but I ran into a group of travellers on my way."

"Like the Red Indians?" I asked curiously, enjoying the distraction from the city surrounding us. In my peripheral vision, I could already see Town Hall burning.

"No, they were nomads of a sort," she explained, her voice calm and soothing against the chaos outside. I focused on the gentle cadence rippling over me like a warm bath. "I found them camping in the woods, living out of oddly shaped carriages that were brightly painted. They called them their vardos and were quite proud of them. When they learned that I was alone, they offered me food and shelter for a time. I learned much of their culture in the weeks I spent with them before they eventually moved on."

"But you didn't stay with them?" I asked.

The corners of Mama's lips lifted into a tiny smile, and her eyes danced with laughter at a memory.

"No," she chuckled softly. "Their spiritual leader, some kind of medicine woman, took me aside one day. She read my palms and did all kinds of strange fancies before looking at me and saying, 'You're

11

still on your Journey. The Spirits don't want you with us.' I asked her why and she explained that my true home lay elsewhere and that I just needed to continue south."

My stomach was churning, and my chest felt tight with nerves by this point. Mama's shocking story didn't help matters, despite her soothing voice. Leila, however, had fallen fast asleep, the rocking of the carriage and Mama's voice lulling her into a deep stupor.

"The Spirits?" I asked, raising a cynical brow. I was starting to doubt Mama's story and wondered if she was simply trying to distract me. "Why haven't you told me this before?"

"You weren't old enough," she said firmly, "and I honestly didn't see the need. It never occurred to me that you would ever have to know."

The carriage jerked underneath us as it hit a hole in the dirt road. I heard Papa swear as it jounced. We were nearly outside the city now, and I started to relax. The edges of town slowly faded behind tall river birch and hickory trees as the road wound its way into a forest.

"And you think I should know now?"

I knew I sounded so doubtful it was nearing rudeness, but my anxiety was too great for tact. Mama never told us fairy tales, so it didn't make sense why she was suddenly sharing a strange story about Spirits and nomads.

Mama's chest swelled as she inhaled deeply.

"Yes," she said, a bit hesitantly. "These people believed in a higher power which they called the Spirits. These Spirits would help them find their true homes and guide them through life. They prayed to them, asking for help, guidance, or any need they required."

"So the Spirits were like God for them?" I asked, trying to grasp what she was talking about. Unlike other southern households, we had never been a devout Christian family, but I knew that God supposedly watched over us, although I did question where He was at the moment.

"Exactly," Mama said, nodding and then lifting her shoulder in a doubtful shrug. "Now, I'm not certain about whether they exist, but I will admit that she had been right in saying I needed to go south. Settling in Atlanta was the best thing that ever happened to me."

She smiled wistfully, her eyes subconsciously looking behind her towards the driver's seat. I knew she was thinking about Papa.

"But why should I know about them?" I asked.

"Ora, I don't know what will happen to us," Mama said solemnly, her eyes holding the fear that her practical voice wouldn't portray. "We might make it to Cherokee County, or we could get separated. Whatever happens, I want you to promise me that you'll take care of Leila until we find each other again."

I knew Mama wasn't playing, but how did the Spirits have anything to do with taking care of Leila? I asked her as much, and she looked puzzled, trying to figure out how to explain.

"When I left the travellers, I kept in mind what the medicine woman had told me," Mama explained. "I didn't have much else to hold onto at the time. I walked and listened to the world around me, as she had told me to do. I listened to my instincts. Nothing unusual happened for many days, and I started to tire of the game. But one day, I reached a crossing where the road divided into two paths. I didn't know which direction was south, and no one was around to ask. I randomly chose a direction, but before I could take a step, a little singing voice came into my head. It said, 'Take the other path.' I'll never forget it for the rest of my life."

"Could you maybe have imagined it?" I asked. "I mean, you must have been starving, dehydrated, all sorts of things. You might have been delirious."

Mama frowned at me crossly.

"I was *not* delirious," she snapped, her nostrils flaring indignantly. "I heard that voice as clearly as if someone had been standing beside me. I obeyed it and have lived a wonderful life ever since."

I reached across and squeezed her hand.

"I'm sorry," I said, my voice softer. "It just took me by surprise."

"Well, I suppose it would," she admitted. "But if something happens, listen for the Spirits. I don't know what I believe, but that voice did come from somewhere. If you and Leila find yourselves alone, remember my story. Open yourself up and listen. Perhaps the voice will guide you too."

Mama's brown eyes were wide and beseeching, pleading with me to understand and listen to her.

"Of course," I murmured.

At that moment, the carriage slowed. Papa swore again, only this time with more fervour. Mama's face paled.

"Ora, wake your sister," she ordered.

I shook Leila gently, not wanting to scare her. She shifted sluggishly, her eyes refusing to open until I shook her harder.

14

"Be quiet now," I whispered, as I could hear men's voices outside. I risked a peek out the window, and my heart froze at the sight of navy blue uniforms. One of them stepped forward, motioning for the carriage to stop.

"Halt there, sir," he ordered. "I'm Captain Beauford of the 51st Ohio regiment, Army of Ohio."

"Union soldiers," I whispered. "What do they want?"

Mama's face was tight as she tried to listen to what was being said. She shook her head at me and put a finger to her lips. All we could hear were the deep mumbles of men's voices, but soon Papa's voice rose above the others.

"I'm Colonel Harding of the 63rd Georgia regiment under Brigadier General Hugh W. Mercer, if you must know," he said in exasperation. "And since it's only my family in this carriage, there's no need not to let us pass."

"Your family is not our concern," Captain Beauford said, his tone stern and unemotional. "We have more interest in you. Being that you're a Confederate Colonel, I'm bound by duty to arrest you and transport you to my superior officer."

My eyes widened. They were going to arrest Papa? Impossible. Papa was a brilliant soldier and fiercely loyal to the Confederacy. He would never be taken without a fight.

"I'm sorry, boy, but you've got the wrong man," I heard Papa say softly, his voice like iron under the polite tone. "Now, let me pass. I want to see my family to safety."

The carriage jerked as Papa tried to move forward but was stopped. I heard the horses snort in agitation.

"I'm afraid we must insist, sir," Captain Beauford snapped firmly. "You can either come willingly, or we can force you."

A still silence overcame all of us. Mama was frozen, her face a mask of intent concentration as she waited for Papa's response to turn this into a fight or peaceful surrender. The outright gall of that soldier caused such a severe rebellion inside me that I almost didn't care what happened. The only reaction could be resistance.

But the other part of me looked at Leila, whose round eyes were full of fear, and I knew I couldn't risk her that way.

As if hearing my thoughts, Papa finally responded, the words spat out as if he disliked their taste.

"We'll go back with you," he said grimly. "I'll talk to your superior officer."

"Women and children out of the carriage first," the soldier said snidely. "I need to make sure there aren't any hidden weapons."

Before Papa could reply, Mama threw the carriage door open and accidentally hit a surprised soldier to the ground.

"There aren't any weapons in here," Mama snapped, standing with her hands on her hips and glaring at the soldiers. The one on the ground desperately scrambled to his feet. "And unless you Yankees weren't brought up with manners, I expect you to accept the word of a lady."

I stayed inside, not planning to move a muscle until Mama told me to. Leila whimpered into my dress, confused by the whole experience.

"We don't mean any disrespect, ma'am," said one of the soldiers gently, obviously trying to keep

Mama calm. "But we have our orders and must see them carried out."

I saw Mama glance up at Papa quickly. Suddenly, Papa climbed down from the carriage and stood between Mama and the soldier.

"I don't care what your orders are," he snapped. "My children are not getting out of this carriage. You're going to have to take our word."

"He must be hiding something with the children!" a soldier barked. "Just get them out of there."

The atmosphere was as tight as a violin's string. All it would take was an outside force to hit that string, and a reaction would happen. I briefly wondered why Papa and Mama were being so stubborn about us getting out of the carriage. It didn't make sense. Leila and I could happily stand outside while they searched the carriage. There was nothing here.

"Ora, Leila, step out, please," Mama said tightly. She maintained her composure, but her face was white with anxiety and anger.

She stood in front of the carriage door but moved to the side as she looked at us. Without conscious thought, I carried Leila out of the carriage to the side of the road, nearly dropping her since my arms were trembling. I decided to set her down. As a soldier stepped toward the carriage, Papa drew his sword.

"I can't let you do that," he said gravely, and before I could even comprehend what was happening, Papa attacked. The soldier skilfully drew his, and the metallic sound of swords clashing rang through the air.

It didn't take more than a few moments before Captain Beauford lost patience entirely and drew his pistol.

"Enough of this!" he roared. "Now, you Confederate bastard, set aside your sword and let us into that carriage, or you'll be responsible for your little girl's death."

I couldn't breathe as I stared at the long-barrelled pistol aimed at Leila's chest. Mama slowly placed her hand into mine and squeezed as she stepped closer to me, placing her warm lips next to my ear.

"When I move forward, take Leila and run," she breathed, then gently kissed my ear lobe. "Remember to listen. I love you."

I couldn't even respond before she had rushed forward into the path of the gun. Her abrupt movement startled Captain Beauford, shifting his aim towards her, and he fired without warning.

Mama crumpled suddenly to the ground.

Papa roared, lunging forward towards Mama with his sword drawn and ready, but a quick soldier's bayonet intercepted him, driving into his belly. My world stopped as Papa's face lost all colour, and he slowly fell.

Leila's scream cut through my frozen panic. I picked her up, tightly clenching her, and took off into the woods silently crying, my head swimming with adrenaline and confusion. I heard footsteps behind me, and I ran faster, nearly tripping over logs and holes. I had no idea where to go or what to do. In the midst of all this chaos, a voice in my head kept repeating, *why?* Why had my parents insisted that the soldiers couldn't enter the carriage? Even to risk dying for it? This realisation nearly made me fall to the ground in despair, but feeling Leila's desperate grip around my neck prevented me from giving in to the temptation. Knowing I couldn't last much longer, I dove into a deep thicket of bracken and waited, praying fervently that the soldier hadn't noticed me.

I saw him stop beside me. I kept my hand over Leila's mouth and prayed as he searched for us. Suddenly, another soldier ran up behind him, breathing heavily.

"Forget them," he panted. "Captain wants you back now. There was a chest of gold under one of the seats."

To my relief, they left quickly, and I exhaled a breath I hadn't realised I'd been holding. Gold? So Mama and Papa had brought gold with us, knowing we would need money. And, of course, they hadn't wanted the Union Army to get it. My parents' stubborn resistance suddenly made sense to me, but it was that same resistance that had ultimately caused their deaths. Had they just let the soldiers take it, that terrible captain wouldn't have threatened Leila, and they'd be alive. Of course, they couldn't have known that was going to happen. I closed my eyes and lowered my head. My heart ached, and I let out an uncontrollable moan. They were gone. They were both gone, and Leila and I were alone. What were we supposed to do without them? I sat for a while in shock, rocking Leila back and forth as I sobbed.

"Where's Mama and Papa?" Leila asked finally, her voice so tiny I nearly didn't hear it through my agonised cries.

"Gone, Sissy," I sobbed. "They're gone."

Leila began crying as well.

Chapter Three

As the sun crept higher into the sky, I knew midday was approaching. We needed to find food and shelter. I stood and tried to think of where we were. The dense forest surrounding us wasn't telling me much. The road seemed to be the logical place to go. I hesitated at the thought of meeting soldiers, but then looked down at Leila and knew she couldn't face the hike through this dense forest full of uneven slopes and thick foliage. I wasn't sure what soldiers would think of two random girls walking down the road wearing high-quality dresses covered in dirt. Surely Captain Beauford's regiment had moved on by now, though we risked notice from others since we did stand out. But we had to take that chance.

"Stay with me, Sissy," I told her, squeezing her hand. "We're going to go find help."

As I scanned the forest, I wondered where exactly this help would be. Even when I found the road, I didn't know which direction to go. Back home was impossible. All of our family and contacts were unapproachable with the city full of Union soldiers. I didn't have the confidence to go back to Atlanta and wade through the chaos with just me and Leila. Even if we did meet someone to help, we would still be at the heart of the conflict. No, I felt it was best to continue Mama and Papa's plan to leave entirely, even if we were now alone.

One step at a time, I finally advised myself. *Find the road.*

Regardless of which direction I chose, there was bound to be an inn along it somewhere. Leila would need to eat while I decided what to do.

"Where are we going?" Leila asked.

"We're going to find the road again," I said. "You and I are going to have an adventure."

This seemed to lift Leila's spirits a bit, and she spritely walked beside me, willing to follow me wherever I led her. Her faith in me created a lump in my throat. I could only hope that I would do what was right for her.

As we stumbled through the forest, trying to find a small trail to follow, I kept my eyes and ears open.

Remember to listen, Mama had said.

I could see her body falling to the ground, and tears stung my eyes. I could hear the clash of steel and picture the bayonet that ended Papa's life. Grief consumed me, blocking all hope of listening or watching for anything. Losing them was too much to bear right now. Leila tugged on my skirts. Her thin brow was furrowed, and she cuddled closer to me.

"Ora, are you alright?" she asked. "I'm tired."

"Yes, I'm fine, Sissy," I assured her, combing her light brown hair with my fingers. "I'm just missing Mama and Papa."

"Me too," she said, and her lip quivered. "I want to go home."

I smiled gently and picked her up, nestling her head into my shoulder and stroking her back.

"I do too, but we can't," I explained soothingly, not wanting to scare her. "We have to find a new home now."

Talking to Leila had a calming effect on me, and I pulled myself together. Somehow knowing that I

21

needed to be there for her allowed me to gather courage.

"Now, let's find that road so we can perhaps find somewhere to eat!" I said, forcing some excitement into my voice to rally our spirits.

After a couple of hours of losing my bearings and backtracking in circles, or so I assumed, I glimpsed a long brown ribbon of road through a clearing and shouted with delight.

"Sissy! There's the road!" I squealed, and she gave me a squeezing hug.

Seeing a sign of civilisation again filled me with hope. When we got to it, I looked either way, but didn't see any signs of life. This made me feel a little better. The experience with Captain Beauford and his men was still too fresh in my mind to handle seeing soldiers. I randomly chose left, praying that it wasn't in the direction of Atlanta. I didn't want to see our old home now.

"How much longer?" Leila whined. "My legs are hurting."

I didn't want to admit it, but so were mine. We weren't accustomed to walking long distances, and we had already been walking for the better part of the day. The sun was starting to kiss the tops of the trees, and I knew dusk would fall in the next few hours.

"Hopefully not much further," I said, sounding more optimistic than I felt.

I knew an inn could be miles away, if there was one at all. I promised myself that if we came across anyone, I would have the courage to ask where we were. My wish came true about an hour later. An elderly, well-to-do couple drove towards us in a light day trap with a grey pony. Leila, always the horse lover, eagerly walked up to the pony, petted it, and gave it kisses, while I talked with the couple.

"Fortunately, there's an inn not too far from here," the woman said, her slow southern drawl calming my nerves. Both hers and her husband's eyes were kind and filled with warm sympathy as they looked at us. "Would you like us to take you? I'm not sure how much further your little sister can walk."

"If it won't cause too much inconvenience, I would be grateful," I said happily, appreciating their concern for Leila.

I decided to trust them, though I was hesitant to tell them about our parents' deaths. Although I couldn't imagine walking many more miles, I also didn't want them to know we were alone and without help. They seemed friendly, but I wasn't sure what they would do if they knew we were orphans.

We climbed up into the trap, squeezing ourselves into the narrow confines of the back. I didn't care how uncomfortable it was. I was sitting at last. Leila saw it as a wonderful adventure and enjoyed bouncing with the light trap's wheels as they ran over the ruts in the road. To my relief, the inn wasn't too far, and the couple were as good as their word, even giving us a small amount of money so we could eat. I thanked them profusely, and they left, the woman watching us with mild concern. She was

23

obviously curious to know what two young girls were doing by themselves on the road but wasn't going to pry. It was clear the couple were from higher society, and I knew that being nosey would be considered rude.

"We're finally here," I breathed in relief. "Let's get something to eat."

The evening was only just approaching as we stepped inside the inn. It was a small structure built of stone and rough-hewn logs. From its appearance, it had been here for at least one hundred years. The logs dominated the inside, lining the ceiling and walls. A cosy fire crackled in a large stone fireplace in one corner, offering warmth to the few rickety wooden tables that sat near it. The rest of the tables were scattered carelessly around the room, filled with a few travellers sipping drinks and playing cards. There was a long bar behind them. A woman at the bar watched us with open-faced curiosity. Her eyes flicked quickly behind us, expecting parents to follow. Seeing none, her eyes narrowed. Unlike the elderly woman, she wasn't as shy about prying.

"What would two young girls be doing out in these parts alone?" she barked. "Come on over here so I can look at you better."

We shuffled over nervously, not liking to be the sudden centre of attention in the small room. The barwoman scrutinised us carefully.

"You're not street urchins, that's for sure. Not with nice clothes like that," she mused. "Though judging by the state of your boots and those pretty petticoats, I'll say you've been walking for miles. And in mud."

Her lip curled slightly at the filthy state of us, and she looked squarely into my eyes.

"No, we're not street urchins," I said firmly and held my head high. I was brought up to have better manners than to slouch and whisper. "We had an accident on the road while travelling with our parents. They were killed. We escaped and managed to find our way here. We're terribly hungry and need something to eat, especially my little sister."

The woman's iron features softened as I spoke. When I finished speaking, her smile was quivering. After a moment, she pulled Leila into a tight embrace.

"Well, I'll be," she said, shaking her head. "Of course, you have to eat. I'll fix you up something right now. You just sit at the bar here where I can keep an eye on you."

The whole room had been listening to us. One of the men sitting at the tables called over to us.

"I'll be happy to keep an eye on the older one," he chuckled. His rough voice rubbed over my skin like sandpaper.

I quickly looked away from him, my stomach clenched with fear at the predatory look he gave me.

"Horace, if you so much as lift one skinny ass-cheek off your seat, I'll personally sweep your corpse outside!" the barwoman bellowed, her deep voice reverberating through the inn. "No one will bother these girls if they want to sleep on my premises."

With her beefy hands on her wide hips, I could tell none of the men wanted to cross her.

"No, ma'am," Horace said quickly, "I wouldn't dream of it."

She huffed under her breath like a bull and then turned a sweet smile to me. I smiled back quickly, not wanting to cross her either.

25

"No worries about me, darlin'," she laughed. "You're safe with me. I can't guarantee the men folk are, but you girls stick with ol' Winnie here, and you'll be fine."

She waved a thick arm towards the bar stools, encouraging us to sit. My legs were burning, and I felt as weak as water. I could only imagine how little Leila must be faring. To my relief, she wasn't complaining, although I assumed that was due to the shock of the day's events. I don't think it had fully registered with either of us that our parents were gone. At the moment, it just felt like a nightmare, and I was soon going to wake up in my warm, soft bed in my familiar room.

"Now, you girls look starving." Winnie's boisterous voice cut into my musing. My stomach growled in appreciation. "I'll just go get two plates and be right back."

A slither of panic crawled up my chest as she left, making me want to curl forward with my arms wrapped tight around myself. I stopped myself, not wanting to alarm Leila. It frightened me to be without Winnie with these strange men, but they ignored us, determined not to cross Winnie further. Fortunately, she was only gone a few moments, and the steaming plate of food consumed all of my thoughts as I ate.

Leila, normally a choosy eater, tucked in. I hadn't realised how famished she must have been, and my stomach sank to my feet. What was I going to do about her? Or us? Tears unwillingly ran down my cheeks, and I started to lose it. Now that I was full, warm, and rested, the shock overwhelmed me, and I burst into sobs. Leila immediately looked frightened and rushed to hug me.

26

"It's alright, Sissy," I assured her, choking back the torrent of tears. "I'm just tired, is all."

Leila frowned, her little pink lip sticking out in stubborn denial. "No, you're sad," she insisted. "What's wrong?"

I didn't get a chance to answer before Winne swept us off our stools in her wide arms and ushered us up the stairs.

"You're run through to the bone," she said firmly. "What you girls need now is a full night's sleep to help settle your nerves. We can figure out a plan in the morning."

Through my tears and shock, I was dimly aware that Leila somehow managed all of this a lot better than me. Perhaps it was because she was young and she hadn't understood everything that had happened.

Winnie's presence was a soothing relief as she helped us undress and gave us clean nightgowns to wear, even though the one for Leila was so long it dragged along the floor. I didn't have to worry about making decisions. It was almost like being with Mama again.

"Thank you," I said, knowing I couldn't possibly show the depth of my gratitude. "I have a little money to pay you for dinner."

Winnie looked at the fifty-cent piece I offered, gave an unladylike snort, and chuckled.

"Your dinner is on me," she said firmly, closing my fist over the money. "Keep it for another time."

Before I could thank her, she turned me around towards the bed. It was a double bed with a thick feather comforter. I looked at it longingly, surprised to see such high-quality bedding in this small establishment. Apparently, Winnie held her hospitality to a high standard, despite her inn's humble appearance. After tucking us in, Winnie stood over us with her hands on her hips, making sure we were comfortable.

"You girls sleep well," she said. "I'm sorry for the loss of your parents."

I nodded quietly, not wanting to face the truth of those words. Hearing them out loud somehow made this entire nightmare a reality. If I stayed quiet, perhaps I could pretend that Mama was only downstairs and would soon come up to our room to say goodnight.

"I'll have a plan made by morning," Winnie said, her voice soft and full of promise.

She sounded so confident that I believed her, and I allowed myself to relax into the bed. Leila spooned her body into me, nestling her legs around mine. I didn't mind since she was like a hot lump of coal, warming me in a way the bed couldn't. Winnie left, blowing out the candles as she went, leaving us in a dark cocoon of silence. The muffled sounds of rough men's voices downstairs distracted me until Leila suddenly whispered.

"Sing Mama's song, Ora." I heard a catch in her voice that told me she was aware that Mama and Papa were dead.

I wrapped my arm around her, laying her head on my chest while I stroked her hair. I didn't mind singing Mama's song. The melody comforted me too. Mama had always sung this song when we were sad or going to bed. It was her special song, and I choked up a few times while singing it. Leila helped, singing the bits she knew.

"I miss her," Leila whimpered, nearly half-asleep.

"Me too," I replied, kissing the top of her head and slowly drifting off to sleep.

Chapter Four

True to her word, by morning, Winnie had made a plan. We would work for her, our pay being room and board until we could figure out where to go.

"I don't mind watching over you two girls as long as you earn your keep," she firmly told me after sending Leila outside to get eggs from the small hatch of chickens she kept. "But I do worry about that little one. She needs a lot more caring for than you do."

I knew Winnie was right, but we left it at that. Not another word was spoken about it for a week, and I wondered if Winnie thought Leila was easier than she had expected. Working for Winnie was hard but undeniably fair. We did our assigned chores, and she never failed to feed us and make sure we had a room. Travellers passing through never paid us much mind, which suited me fine. I didn't feel like talking to anyone, and Leila was abnormally shy with strangers now, though one could hardly blame her. If soldiers came through, Leila cried in fear and raced to our room, shirking her chores completely until they were gone. I appreciated Winnie's tolerance for this. She got the full story out of me that next morning, so she understood why Leila was scared of them. I wasn't entirely comfortable with the soldiers either, but I could tell the difference between a Unionist and a Confederate. Any man in uniform terrified Leila.

I had settled comfortably into our new routine, doing chores diligently to keep my mind occupied and not think about our parents. Leila was always with Winnie doing her chores so she could be watched over, so I often worked alone. I was sweeping the floor in the front room when I heard it. It came from nowhere, my mind blissfully blank as I focused on the broom bristles scratching along the floor.

"It's time to leave," a voice sang with an odd melodic chime that didn't make it male or female.

I jumped and looked around, searching for the voice, but the room was empty, and it was too early for travellers to come in. My heart slowed down as I told myself I must have been hearing things, but the voice had been so clear and loud in my head that I doubted myself. A voice talking in my head. Why did that sound so familiar? I put the broom down and concentrated. Suddenly, I remembered. Mama.

Remember to listen, she had said.

I sat down on a chair, my head swimming too fast to keep on my feet. I must have heard someone from outside. Yes, that was it, but it was far too early. Could Mama's story actually be true? I rubbed my hands over my face, and stood up.

"Who are you?" I asked the room aloud, feeling mildly foolish and grateful no one was around to hear.

Silence. I waited a few moments, but nothing came. That settled it. I had thought of Mama, and my subconscious had conjured this imaginary voice. I liked this practical thought. I picked up my broom and got back to sweeping. It was nothing more than my imagination.

Yet, Mama's words lingered as I swept, and I thought back to our last conversation. She wasn't one for telling fancy stories for the sake of it...but Spirits?

When I finished sweeping, I went into the kitchen to ask Winnie what my next chore was. She was busy preparing breakfast. I smiled as I entered the kitchen area. Leila was standing on a footstool in front of the stove, stirring a steaming pot of boiling porridge.

"Look, Ora, I'm cooking!" she crowed happily, making Winnie and I laugh.

"Yes, and doing a fine job too." Winnie beamed, her face red from the oven's heat. "She'll make a proper cook yet, your sister."

"What do you need me to do next?" I asked, wondering how much cleaner this inn could get as the thought of Spirits was pushed aside.

Day in and day out, I would clean it from top to bottom, all to start over again the next day. Though I was happy to have a place to stay, the constant work was tiresome, but I appreciated Winnie's help too much to complain.

"Nothing at the moment," Winnie said, making my brows rise in surprise. "But I do need to have a word with you after the breakfast service is done."

I nodded, setting the broom down in its corner. A niggle of intuition was settling into my gut. Maybe this had to do with the voice talking to me. Although I wasn't convinced it had existed, it seemed coincidental that it had come at this moment. Winnie didn't take the time to have a word with me unless it was something serious.

Fortunately, the breakfast service didn't take long. We only had a few guests, though one couple intrigued me. I enjoyed talking with them as I brought their breakfast. They were a young couple, probably only in their mid-twenties. The woman's thick fur coat over her silk dress and the man's new suit and hat made it clear they had money. When asked where they were going, their answer astounded me.

"We're on our way to Charleston to make sail for Europe," the woman told me, her voice light and charming.

"How lovely," I replied. "Where in Europe?"

"Well, not just one place," the man cut in, laughing jovially.

His wide, drawn-out accent was a bit different than his wife's, who was American, but I couldn't place it.

"Europe is simply on the way to our final destination," he explained. "I'm originally from Australia. Ever hear of it?"

I shook my head, dumbfounded. I had only heard of Europe, and in all honesty, I didn't know much about it.

"It sounds far away," I said lamely, picturing some exotic shore similar to what Robinson Crusoe would have found.

"It is, which is why Europe is only our first stop," his wife continued. "We then have to go on over Africa and Asia before making sail to Australia, but I don't mind since I want to see Europe anyway."

I stared at them, my eyes wide with wonder at the sound of such a trip. Their words were nearly incomprehensible to me.

"My goodness, what brought you all the way to the south here?" I asked, curiosity overcoming manners.

"Cotton business, of course," the man replied, waving a careless hand as if that should be obvious. I excused myself and left them to their meal. I wondered briefly why such a well-off couple would stop by a small, rustic inn and not at a finer hotel. The Cow's Crossing, as the inn was named, was only a simple inn designed for the road-weary traveller. This couple seemed to be used to travel and had money to make plans. Surely they could have found a nicer establishment in Atlanta. My footsteps slowed as I realised that Atlanta wasn't exactly the safest place right now. Perhaps that had stopped them.

"Come here, Ora," Winnie said from the hall to the kitchen. "I saw you talking with that couple. I have something to tell you."

"Where's Leila?" I asked suddenly, realising that she wasn't with Winnie like she usually was.

"I sent her upstairs to dust the furniture," Winnie replied quickly. "We need to talk about her."

Something in her tone made me go pale. There was something wrong.

"What is it? Is she doing her chores alright? I can always help her more if you want," I said urgently. I didn't want Winnie to send us away.

Out of nowhere, the melodic voice snuck into my head.

"It's time to leave."

Hush, I ordered it firmly, *not now*.

I was trembling, so Winnie had me sit on a footstool. Between worrying about what Winnie would say and the mysterious voice, my nerves were failing me. It didn't take much these days for me to become emotional.

"No, you're both fine workers," Winnie assured me, but she watched me carefully. Her tone was grave and soft, making my skin prickle. "Ora, I've been happy to care for you girls, but we both know it can't last forever. I'm not in the position to raise two girls, much less one as young as Leila."

I nodded, knowing Winnie had always been concerned about Leila's age.

"And you're nearly grown," she continued, almost apologetic. "You need to be going to find a man. My life is here in this inn. It's not a life for a young girl."

"We help you, though," I argued, but I knew it was useless. I sighed heavily, my energy seeping onto the floor.

"And it's been a great help," Winnie said gently, wrapping me into a warm hug and then setting me back and squeezing my shoulders.

"But an opportunity has presented itself that I can't ignore."

My ears perked at this. So she wasn't going to just send us on our way? She had a plan!

"That wealthy couple you talked to took a shine to Leila when we were serving dinner last night," Winnie explained. "They asked me about her, and I told them your story. Well, they have no children of their own and took pity, so they offered to give her a home."

My eyes widened in amazement. New parents! And wealthy ones at that. I smiled, a bubble of hope building in my chest as I pictured the possibilities. We'd travel the world with them and end up in all those exotic countries they had been talking about. My smile widened.

"That sounds wonderful," I said happily. "We'd have a real home again."

Winnie shook her head. "They want a young child to raise."

My bubble burst, leaving me deflated and cold. Even my voice was flat and toneless as I replied. "Only Leila? But I take care of her. She's my sister."

"Ora," Winnie said firmly, "you don't have to take care of her anymore. She'll have parents that can give her a better life than you ever could. You need the freedom to go find a new life for yourself. You don't need the worry of raising a child at sixteen years of age. Leila will be given every opportunity for happiness."

Her words slowly sank in, filtering through the heartbreak at the thought of Leila and I being separated.

"I hear you," I finally said, nearly cutting her off, my head whirling. "I need to talk with them. And Leila."

Winnie nodded and led me out to the front. The couple were at their table, and Leila was sitting on the woman's knee, giggling with delighted laughter at the peacock feather on the woman's hat tickling her nose.

"Ora!" Leila cried when she saw me and scampered towards me. "The pretty lady said I could go live with them!"

My heart broke. I uncontrollably cried out and burst into tears. I tried to smile through the pain. Leila's bright eyes were shining for the first time in weeks. I knew Winnie was right; I just didn't like it. My life was too unstable to make it fair for Leila. I didn't even know where I would go or how to survive. Leila had a chance to make a life for herself and be raised by proper parents.

"That's wonderful, Sissy," I said, lifting her into a tight hug as I hid my tears in her hair. "You're going to be so happy."

I put her down and looked over at the couple.

"We'll take good care of her," the man said warmly. "My wife and I have wanted a child for a long time, and it seems God's providence that Leila just appeared out of nowhere. I thank you for letting us raise her."

I wanted to yell at him. How dare he assume he could just take what was left of my family, my world. But in my heart, I knew that Leila's future was more important.

"You'd better take care of her," I said, forcing a polite tone laced with warning.

By this time, Leila could tell I wasn't happy and was frowning at me.

"I like them," she told me. "We'll be happy with them."

I knelt down to look into her eyes, twirling her hair in my fingers.

"Only you, Sissy," I said softly, and she started to shake her head, but I stopped her. "I'm grown up now. I have to go find a place to live. These nice people are going to be your new Mama and Papa. They're going to take you on so many adventures. When you grow up, you can find me again."

Tears fell down Leila's cheeks as she registered what I was saying.

"But you're my sister," she sniffled. "We are always together."

"And we will be again," I insisted, more for my sake than hers. "I'll look for you when I can, and you look for me. One day we'll find each other."

It was the best solace I could give her. To make her believe that we'd meet again one day when I knew it would be impossible. She was going to live in some exotic place, whereas I…well, I didn't even know yet.

"I love you, Ora," Leila said, burying her head into my chest and wrapping her arms around my neck.

"I love you too, Sissy," I whispered.

I stood up, carrying Leila in my arms as I walked to the woman.

"She's yours," I said woodenly, passing Leila over to her.

The woman looked surprised as she took Leila, obviously unaccustomed to holding children, but delighted.

"Thank you," she said gently. "I can't express how grateful we are for your understanding. We wish you the best of luck finding your next home, and as a gesture of our gratitude, we'd like to offer you compensation."

I frowned at the bag of coins the man was holding out to me and shook my head, offended at the gesture.

"I can't take that," I said. "It would be like I was selling her."

I vaguely remembered Papa buying a mother and her child when I was little. At the time, I hadn't thought much about the transaction. Now an odd twist of conscience made me realise what it would be like to accept money for Leila. She wasn't livestock any more than that mother and her child.

"Please," he insisted, "it would be nothing of the sort. Although we can't provide you with a home, we would like to help you find a new one."

Phrased like that, I could see what he meant. A part of me still bridled at the thought that they didn't want me. That I was too old for them. But it felt wrong to exchange Leila's opportunity for money.

"I won't take it," I said firmly. "Please, use it to buy Leila a new dress and shoes."

He nodded reluctantly and then looked over at Winnie, who had come to stand beside me for support.

"We'd best be off," he said slowly. "We have to make good time to reach Charleston."

I gave Leila one last hug, not caring that I nearly squashed the woman to do it.

"Remember me," I told her firmly. "Remember Mama's song. Remember to listen."

I didn't even know what I was saying, but Mama's last words were all I could think of. Leila nodded solemnly, but I knew at four years old, she wouldn't remember. The couple left with her, and I collapsed in tears, holding onto Winnie's skirts.

Chapter Five

"*It's time to leave.***"**

I growled at the voice, determined to ignore it. It was a few days later, and Winnie had given me time to compose myself and make a plan before I headed off on my own. The voice had become more incessant since Leila had left, and I heard it so often that it didn't surprise me anymore. It also irritated me that it said the same phrase repeatedly. My responses were to tell it to be quiet or growl at it, as I did now. Not only did the voice irk me since I already knew I had to leave, but it frightened me. It was creepy to hear a voice coming from nowhere, no matter how gentle or soothing it sounded. I scrubbed the table I was cleaning harder, fury feeling better than fear.

Go away, I thought harshly, too annoyed to bother talking back. *You're annoying. Where am I supposed to go anyway?*

I didn't know why I was bothering to respond to it at all, but my patience had snapped.

"*North*," it sang.

I stopped scrubbing, frozen at the new word and that it was talking back to me.

"Where?" I whispered, my lips numb with fright and every limb trembling.

Silence. I took a deep breath, and repeated the question in my head.

"*North*," it echoed.

I scoffed under my breath in irritation and smacked the rag against the table.

"Of course, you'd repeat yourself," I grumbled. "Heaven forbid you be specific."

Suddenly, I was blinded by an image flashing across my eyes. The inn disappeared completely, and I was staring at a bustling city lined with tall buildings and full of more people than I had ever seen. At the end of the street, I could vaguely see a large bridge supported by multiple arches, and so long, I couldn't see the end of it. The image disappeared, and I sat back down, my legs like water.

A city in the north, I thought, and heard bells chime. I supposed this meant the Spirits were pleased.

And that's what this voice had to be, I reasoned. Mama mentioned that the travellers had called them Spirits. She told me to listen out for them. If she'd heard them, then they're real.

I kicked myself for not taking her words more seriously, but at the time, I hadn't known I would need them so much. Now I was scrambling to remember her story and the voice she'd heard. I remembered she had told me to open myself up and listen to my instincts. I assumed that when I did, then the Spirits would come.

"Alright," I said softly. "I'll listen."

I didn't know if I was telling the Spirits or Mama's memory, but in saying the words, I felt a bit better. Ever since Leila had left, I'd felt more alone than ever. Winnie was a comforting presence, but I knew my time with her was temporary. Now I had a new presence to guide and support me. Not only that, but they also gave me a destination. I knew that as long as I kept myself open to them, they would guide me the rest of the way. I simply had to make the first step and begin my journey.

After telling Winnie where I planned to go but not my reason for it, I left, carrying the small luggage case she had given me. Inside was a change of clothes, some food, and a little money to support me when I got there.

"Good luck, Ora," she said wistfully. "Lots of jobs up north, so it's a smart place to go. You're bound to find something."

I thanked her one last time and headed off down the road. It felt surreal knowing I would never see her again. Despite her rough demeanour and high standards of cleanliness, Winnie had been my saving grace. But the intriguing prospect of being guided to a new home tempered my sadness. It was nearly October, and the bitter north wind was snaking its way south. It blew through the trees, rattling the leaves above my head. I stopped, instinctively listening to the wind. I knew from the sharp chill that it was a northern wind that carried winter along with it.

"*Follow the north wind,*" my Spirits sang.

I smiled, happy to hear their voice. Instead of feeling irritated and pushing them away, I opened myself further, embracing their guidance. I had lost everything in my life; my home, my family, and any future I had imagined. It was a warm comfort to embrace something that helped give me guidance.

"Whatever you say," I agreed, and turned to face the bitter wind and head in the way it came from.

How long I would travel didn't matter to me. Guided by the Spirits, time seemed endless, but the journey wasn't frightening. I had a constant companion, ready to answer me if I had a question. My Spirits led me to every inn, helped me avoid danger, and made sure I never failed to head in the right direction. It also felt comforting to know that, in a way, I was walking in my mother's footsteps, guided by the same Spirits that had led her to Atlanta, only I was heading in the opposite direction. I asked travellers I met at the inns about the big city the Spirits had shown me, describing the details I knew, and ask if it was familiar to them. Based on their answers, I finally learned which big city I was heading for.

"Sounds like you're describing New York," one traveller told me. "That bridge could be High Bridge since you say it's so large. Biggest bridge to be built in the last two hundred years."

It seemed like a good guess, and my Spirits weren't protesting, so to New York I would go and find what life awaited me there. But I knew I wasn't going there alone. In my soul, I could feel that my Spirits would be with me on every journey throughout my life, as I knew now, they must have been for Mama. But there was always one prayer I would send to them every day.

Take care of Leila, I'd pray to them, *and let us meet again.*

Then I'd pick up my luggage and follow the north wind.

For seven days, I followed the Spirits, spending the money Winnie had given me as sparingly as I could when I needed to stop for the night. Some inns allowed me to wash dishes or work in some way for my board, which helped me save money.

Fortunately, it seemed the Spirits always guided me to safe inns where other means of earning money for a night weren't offered to me. I was still in Confederate territory, which was comforting. After enquiring, I had been told by the innkeeper that I was now in Orange County, North Carolina.

"How long until I reach New York?" I had asked.

The innkeeper's eyes had widened.

"At least another two weeks, maybe a bit more," she had replied. "Especially if you're only on foot."

I wasn't sure how I would face the north being a southerner. I set down my fork at the breakfast table and sighed heavily. The eggs I had been eating felt like lead in my stomach. The thought of the north made my stomach churn so violently with nerves that I felt nauseous.

For a week, I had thought of little else except simply travelling in the direction the Spirits wanted me to go and surviving from inn to inn. I hadn't let myself think ahead towards my destination since the thought of any Yankee made my blood freeze. My boots were nearly run through to the sole, and I had several blisters from the days of walking from morning to evening. I was weary. My legs felt shaky every time I started off, and it was getting harder to lift my luggage case. I knew I couldn't last much longer like this.

Despite knowing I would be hungry later, my nerves wouldn't let me eat any more. I carried my plate to the kitchen, knowing the innkeeper would be there. I thanked her, paid for my night's lodging, and went up the stairs to my room to pack. After a few minutes, since I had very little belongings, I descended the stairs and left. The wind was picking up, and it was getting chillier. I wrapped the thick shawl Winnie had provided me a little closer around my neck, though over the past days, it had become more worn and thin. It was only made of light cotton instead of wool. The weather worried me. It was nearing mid-October, and the weather was getting more unpredictable.

With a weary groan, I set off down the isolated road that continued to be surrounded by forest, following wheel ruts and trying to avoid puddles. My soles were now so thin that one step into any moist mud soaked my stockings right through. With one eye on the dark clouds and one on the road, I was too preoccupied with present concerns to think ahead to future ones. After a couple of hours, my luck ran out. A heavy downpour cascaded from the ominous clouds, soaking me instantly.

"Thunderation!" I shouted angrily, putting the shawl over my head in vain. My luggage case whacked my head for my troubles.

I didn't curse very often, but at this present moment, I didn't care who heard me. The rain was torrential and relentless. After the first few moments of frenzied panic at getting wet, I realised that it hardly mattered. I couldn't find shelter from this. Everything was soaked in a matter of seconds, even areas under trees. I stumbled along, slipping in mud every few feet. The daylight had dimmed with the darkening clouds, and it was getting harder to see the road.

"Consarn it," I muttered, the cursing making me feel better. "Goshdarn storm, making my life harder than it is. And where are you, Spirits? What am I supposed to do now?"

I shouted this last at the sky, staring up accusingly. My anger had clouded over all reason and self-awareness. I was tired, sore, hungry, and downright miserable. I was also near tears with frustrated exhaustion. Suddenly, I heard a sound through the roaring wind and rain. The rattle of wheels bumped along the road. I looked behind me towards the sound and squinted through my wet lashes.

An old wagon filled with barrels and wooden crates covered with burlap rolled slowly towards me. It was driven by a lone man, hunched over, covered with a large woollen blanket to block the rain. Relief at seeing a sign of possible help outweighed any qualm I had about being alone with a strange man. I waved my arm high, hoping he could see me.

Thank you. I sent a mental message to the Spirits. In the recesses of my mind, I heard bells, so I figured they were pleased. I had learned that talking to them out loud didn't work. They would only respond to my thoughts.

I pondered over this in the few seconds it took for the wagon to stop next to me. After a brief second of hesitation, I shouted up to the man driving. I wasn't in a position to be picky about who could help me.

"Pardon me, sir, but could you please allow me to accompany you?" I asked as politely as I could, despite having to shout up at him like an ill-bred street mongrel.

The shape of him nodded, and he reached out a hand and helped me climb up beside him. When I saw the brown colour of his hand, I was struck with shock. This must be a slave heading back home with that week's supplies. A part of me was relieved, since this meant we'd be travelling to a well-to-do southern family, which would be familiar to me.

"My name is Miss Ora Harding," I said as the wagon moved on again. "What do they call you?"

The man glimpsed at me with widened eyes and grunted as he helped to cover my head with part of the large woollen blanket.

"I'm Briton Corn," he replied briskly. "Why are you alone? Especially in this."

He waved a hand to encompass the storm. I was too taken aback by his response to answer right away. Briton didn't seem like a common slave name, much less Corn. His direct way of speaking was certainly not like a slave. I started to get apprehensive about who my travelling companion was.

"I'm on my way to New York," I said, shifting uneasily on the hard wagon bench.

"All that way?" Briton replied, his tone both disapproving and surprised. "That's a long way for a young woman on her own."

I shrugged, not wanting to get into the details. I decided to keep the conversation light and impersonal.

"Thank you for assisting me," I said gratefully. "I don't know how much longer I could have been out here."

"I wouldn't leave a dog out in this weather, much less people," he grunted. "I'm going back to my village, Little Texas, with supplies. You can stay with my people until the weather is clear enough again to travel."

His people? Nerves circled my stomach again, and I swallowed a knot in my throat. What on earth kind of man was he? Brown-skinned, but not a slave. At least, not a current one anyway. Could he be a former escaped slave who had a kind of group he was staying with? My neighbours would discuss such groups before. I had heard they were wild and not friendly with strangers, possibly even dangerous! Although Briton didn't exactly seem dangerous, it scared me a little to think I was being carried into a large group of former slaves.

"Who are your people?" I asked timidly.

"The Occaneechi," he said dryly. I knew he could hear how nervous I was.

I was too shocked to care what he thought of me. I was heading towards a tribe of Red Indians. Although I was drenched and cold, I started to also tremble with fear. It was raining too hard for me to see Briton in detail, but I was surprised he was driving a wagon. When I thought of Red Indians, I envisaged half-naked men living off the land with bows and arrows. Even though the heavy rain prevented me from looking closely at him, Briton seemed to be dressed in a normal cotton shirt and trousers. I took a deep breath.

The Spirits would not lead me into any danger, I tried to convince myself. *They obviously sent this man, so trust them.*

As my heart pounded and I squeezed my skirt nervously, I knew I wasn't doing a good job convincing myself. Briton stayed quiet, obviously not being the chatty kind. In a way, this suited me since I was too scared and tired to be able to hold much conversation anyway. Added to that, the storm was incessant and wild, making conversation difficult. Briton was most likely waiting until we were in better conditions before asking questions.

I settled as comfortably as I could and focused on being grateful that my legs were resting, despite the sharp pain of blisters and my toes starting to cramp in the cold. As scared and uncertain as I was, I appreciated that someone had come along. I couldn't have gone on further alone. Briton seemed kind, so hopefully his people were as well. I stared straight ahead through the curtain of rain and waited for what Little Texas would bring.

Chapter Six

After a couple of hours, we arrived at a strange kind of settlement. The rain had subsided to a mere drizzle, and I could see more clearly. A narrow path ran between large domes that looked like dwellings. They were covered by grass, brush, and even animal hides, and a large log building stood regally in the near distance. The settlement was in a large meadow, with fenced gardens randomly placed behind the odd dwellings further off. Dark forest surrounded us, but I could see craggy mountain tops peeking above the line of trees. Sudden shrill cries nearly made me scream as dozens of men, women, and children all ran towards the wagon.

"You're here!" they cried in a strange mixture of English and simple trills, a language I had never heard.

I sat still, trying not to attract attention until I could get a feel for what this chaotic crowd was like. Briton laughed at something someone said, and then he turned to me.

"This is Little Texas. I will take you to the Iⁿya, our women. They will help you."

Briton hadn't said more than a few words to me in the past couple of hours, so I was taken aback, not to mention completely overwhelmed by the Red Indians surrounding the wagon. The people were dressed in a variety of odd clothing, some in normal attire of skirts, blouses, or trousers with shirts, and others in deerskin. Some were even wearing a combination of both.

"Step away," Briton commanded, waving his hand at the eager children. "Give the woman space."

I wasn't sure I wanted to leave the safety of the wagon. My eyes were wide with amazement as I dropped to the ground. The people stared at me, their own eyes wide with open curiosity. Only a few of the women had their eyes narrowed with suspicion and their arms crossed. I hoped they wouldn't be the ones to help me.

"Follow me," Briton said, placing a soft hand on my elbow to guide me.

I was startled at his touch, but followed readily. My knees knocked together as I walked like a newborn colt. Scents of venison and roasted vegetables drifted across my nose, and my stomach growled in appreciation. I could smell the acrid scent of burning wood and ash from an open fire. I had been right about the domes. Women and children peeked out from the arched doorways, much like our nosey neighbours had done in Atlanta from their windows.

"These are your homes?" I asked curiously.

"They are wigwams," Briton explained, nodding. "They keep us warm, dry, and a place for privacy. A home doesn't need more than that."

I cocked an eyebrow at that but remained silent. Upon closer inspection, and because he had taken off his woollen blanket, I could now see fully what Briton looked like. He appeared as any lower to middle-class man might dress, with faded brown trousers, a light cotton shirt, and stretched suspenders. However, the similarity ended with the club of long black hair tied behind his head, and a strange necklace of beads and feathers draped around his neck. He was also wearing deer-skin shoes that were like women's slippers. The long-sleeved flowing cotton shirt he wore didn't look warm, but the damp chill in the air didn't seem to bother him. I, however, was soaked to the bone and frozen to the core. We arrived at a wigwam, and Briton motioned me in. I stepped inside the dimly lit interior, having the strangest sensation of feeling like I was playing a childhood game.

"She needs a fire," Briton said, and I suddenly noticed a woman sitting in the back, staring at us open-mouthed.

"Of course," she replied, and motioned me to sit on the dirt floor next to the smouldering pile of logs in the centre of the wigwam. "What is your name?"

"Ora," I replied, shivering uncontrollably as the warmth reached me.

"You are welcome here," the woman replied smoothly. "I'm Sarah Corn, Briton's wife."

"Thank you," I said, rubbing my stiff hands together. "I truly appreciate your hospitality."

Sarah studied me carefully, not trying to hide her curiosity. I watched her eyes travel over me, taking in my worn dress, muddy boots, and threadbare shawl. I knew I had to look as pathetic as I felt. Briton lightly touched Sarah's shoulder and gave his head a short jerk towards me.

"I thought the I^{n}ya could help her get settled for a time," he told her, and she nodded. "I have to go speak with the men."

Sarah squeezed his hand on her shoulder, and Briton left. She gave me a small smile and gently placed more logs onto the fire. Since she had felt comfortable studying me so openly, I did the same to her. She didn't seem to mind—almost expected it. She was a short, stout woman and very graceful. Her attire was the same as many of the women I'd seen. Cotton blouses and skirts, accessorized with bright, beaded jewellery that was foreign to me. She also wore the same deerskin slippers that her husband wore. Her jet-black hair was braided back into a tight ponytail that neatly kept the strands out of her eyes. I self-consciously stroked my own hair, feeling how greasy and unkempt it was. I hadn't had a chance to have a proper bath for a week. I had never felt comfortable enough in the inns to do more than a bit of spot washing.

"You're a Confederate," Sarah said, surprising me with the random statement.

"Yes," I said, a bit proudly. I saw no reason to lie. "My father was a Confederate Colonel before he...died."

I nearly choked on the last word, but managed to get it out. I still couldn't think of my parents' deaths without crying. Sarah kindly squeezed my shoulder, her eyes sympathetic.

"You need Ya^{n}hi," she stated, and stood to retrieve a small canteen from a deerskin jacket hanging from a peg. "It will refresh you."

I didn't know what the canteen held, but I knew it was liquid, and that was all that mattered. I was thirstier than I realised. To my relief, it was nothing but water. Sarah was right; the coolness of it awakened me, and I felt remarkably better.

"What language are you speaking?" I asked curiously, handing the canteen back to her. I was relieved that Briton and Sarah predominately spoke English, but their use of foreign words confused me.

"Siouan," Sarah replied, sitting down beside me. "It's the traditional language of the Occaneechi, though we speak English fluently when necessary."

"How did you know I was a Confederate?" I asked.

Sarah raised her brows in surprise as if this should be quite obvious.

"Your accent is from the deep south," she said slowly. "It's easy to tell."

I nodded and shrugged, accepting that I should have been aware of this. My brain must have been more muddled than I thought.

"A few members of the Occaneechi joined the Confederacy," Sarah went on. "Although many of them are from the Catawba tribe. The rest of us try to stay out of the war, but it's difficult not to be affected."

I frowned, concerned by the shadowed look on her face as she thought about the war. It had never once occurred to me that the Red Indians would be affected.

"I'm sorry," I said softly, though I wasn't sure why I felt the need to apologise. The war was hardly my own personal doing, but I did feel somewhat responsible since it was my people fighting it.

Sarah smiled, lifting her shoulders in a shrug that plainly said, 'What can you do?'

"We can talk later," she said firmly, standing up and taking my shawl off my shoulders. "You need new clothing and food."

My body felt warm and limber again, but she was right. My clothes were destroyed, particularly my boots. Sarah cocked an eyebrow as she pulled them off my feet, looking at the holes in the soles and the hobnails sticking out from the bottom. I wanted to protest that I could undress myself, but her no-nonsense approach and swift movements prevented me.

"I'll give you moccasins," she said, clucking her tongue in disapproval. "These will not do. I might be able to save your dress, but you'll need a new shawl."

She continued to undress me, taking off each layer of shirt, bodice, and dress until I was only in my chemise. She even removed my stockings, peeling them off since they were still wet and stuck to my skin. I felt completely naked, which embarrassed me. I hadn't undressed like this in front of someone since Phibe, but she hadn't been a stranger.

"Where is your corset?" she asked, puckering her eyebrows in confusion.

"I left it in an inn a few days ago," I said, wrapping my arms around my shoulders, both from chilliness and modesty. "It's hard to walk in for a long time."

Raised eyebrows were her only reply as she continued to work with my clothing, discarding the shawl in a corner to be used for rags, and hanging the rest on a long wooden pole that hung across the wigwam over the fire. I looked around the large wigwam.

It's certainly a strange way of living, I mused, though Briton had a point. It had everything one would practically need.

The structure was held up by thick wooden sticks shaped into a dome, which could be seen on the walls. All of the belongings and benches faced the fire in the centre. A long wooden bed covered with straw and animal hides was placed against the furthest wall. Bits of pottery, baskets, blankets, and tools were hung on little pegs on the walls. Small logs were stacked under the bed and along the wall to my left. As primitive as it was, I was surprised to find that it also felt quite cosy. There was something comforting about being in such a small space. However, this comforting feeling dissipated when Sarah turned her attention back to me.

"I'll need this as well," she said, pointing to my chemise, which was still quite damp. I didn't want to take it off.

"It can dry on me," I argued feebly, not wanting to be completely naked in front of her.

Sarah seemed to sense this and her brows fell heavily.

"We're both women," she assured me, reaching towards my chemise. I took an involuntary step back, and she smiled. "Don't worry. You don't have anything I haven't seen before."

I was shaking with nerves but nodded, taking it off myself and then immediately wrapping my arms around my chest. Sarah shook her head and chuckled as she hung the chemise next to the rest of my clothes.

"I have a spare dress you can borrow," she said. "It's not what you're used to, but it will warm you faster than white people's clothes."

Stripped of all clothing, I was colder than ever, so I wasn't too picky about what she had. However, to my shock, she held out a deerskin dress covered with tassels and white beads.

"It's only this," she said, placing it over my head and allowing it to drop over me. "There aren't any undergarments."

For a moment, I was struck speechless at the fact that I was wearing Red Indian clothes. Nothing could have felt more foreign to me. I stroked the soft leather. It was fairly thin but surprisingly heavy and warm. Without anything underneath, I could move more freely. I still felt a bit naked but certainly more dry and comfortable.

"It's nice," I managed to say, which made Sarah laugh.

"It's different for you, I know," she said, playing with the tassels. "But it's what you need for now. I miss wearing it sometimes."

I cocked my head. "Why did you ever stop?"

Sarah's face fell.

"Times changed for my people," she said simply. "We had to adapt to white man's ways to survive. The way we dress, our religion...all had to change."

She turned away, abruptly ending the subject, so I didn't pursue it. I felt like an intruder, and it reminded me of when I would go near the slaves' quarters when I was little. Our slaves knew their manners and would only treat me with respect, but I had felt unwelcome when I went near their quarters, even as a little girl. I knew that I was unwanted in the one place that was their private space. I learned quickly never to go near their quarters again, and hadn't felt that same feeling until this moment. I sat down and held my hands towards the fire again. I hadn't thought of that time as a little girl in years.

"Come, we'll go meet the others," Sarah said calmly. I was relieved that she didn't sound upset. "You still need to eat, and the I^{n}ya will be curious to see you."

I stood up and followed her, reluctant to leave the safe space of the wigwam. I didn't know what to expect when meeting the other women, but I felt alien as we walked through the maze of wigwams and people. Many stared at me, curious but not hostile. Some seemed wary, others just indifferent. I was a white stranger, but obviously not their first.

"We farm our own land," Sarah said, gesturing towards a large field as we walked past. "My family, the Corns, and the Jeffries own the largest sections. We also have a schoolhouse where we teach our children."

She pointed to the wooden building I had seen before. As we got closer, I saw it was a single-room log schoolhouse.

"Your children go to school?" I asked in amazement, and flushed with embarrassment at how condescending I sounded. Sarah's lips curled into an amused grin, and she raised an eyebrow at me.

"We are God-fearing people, Ora," she said, just shy of accusing. "We have learned how to read and write, and will continue to teach our children to do so."

As if she felt the need to prove this to me, she led me to another wooden building I instantly recognised as a church. I was beginning to feel incredibly small and humiliated by how much I had assumed about the Red Indians. Everything I had read or heard about them was proving to be untrue. Although, I realised now that my high-society friends gossiping over their tea were hardly reliable sources of information. This thought made my cheeks burn with shame, but Sarah didn't notice, continuing to show me her village.

"This is our church, Jeffries Cross," Sarah explained proudly.

It wasn't a terribly large church, but it was structurally solid and well-kept. A plain cross sat atop the roof. I stared at it for a while. It had been a long time since I had attended a service. My family had been Christians but not overly devout. There were the odd Sundays we would skip services.

"I didn't realise you were Christians," I admitted sheepishly. "I'm sorry I know so little."

Sarah chuckled and shook her head. "Of course you don't. You have never met us before."

She continued on, and I followed, my head spinning. I was starting to question everything I had ever known. What else had I assumed was the truth but was only a falsehood?

"Here we are," Sarah said. We were standing outside a large wigwam, much larger than hers and Briton's. "This is where the I^{n}ya meet to talk and work."

We stepped inside and faced a group of women sitting in a circle around the fire, weaving baskets, sewing clothes, and stripping hide. I was relieved not to see any of the women from earlier who had been looking at me suspiciously. The group of women stopped talking the minute we entered, eyes wide with astonishment as they looked at me. I knew I had to be a surprising spectacle as a white woman in a deerskin dress and moccasins.

"This is Ora," Sarah said, introducing me. "She's a Confederate staying with Briton and me until she recovers from her travels."

The oldest woman, probably around her mid-fifties, stood and nodded in greeting.

"Mecou, you're welcome here," she said. "It sounds like you have a story to tell us. Sit down, and let us hear about your travels."

59

My heart started thumping nervously as every eye looked at me. Apparently, my story would be told, whether I liked it or not.

Chapter Seven

I sat down on one of the wooden, hide-covered benches near the wall. I didn't even know where to begin. Sarah had casually wandered over to the pot hanging above the fire and scooped a stew-like substance into a bowl. Handing this to me now, she gave me an encouraging smile and sat down. I ate before speaking. This apparently was socially acceptable, since the other women patiently continued their work, watching me as they waited. The stew was a mix of venison, corn, and squash, and was quite good. I was also ravenous, which made it taste even better.

After I finished the bowl, I set it aside and decided to share what I could. I didn't want to mention the Spirits' part in this if I could help it. I felt it would sound too absurd. I also didn't know how the Red Indian culture would interpret them and thought it best to play it safe.

"I come from Atlanta, Georgia," I began, and all eyes turned towards me at once to listen.

"That's a long way from here," the oldest woman said in surprise. "You've been travelling a long while."

"Yes," I continued, "I've been walking for the past seven days. That's why Sarah let me borrow her clothes. Mine need tending to."

"I wondered why she was dressed like that!" one of the women chuckled, turning to Sarah.

Everyone shared a moment of laughter, and I patiently waited. I had to admit that it was pretty ironic that I was the only woman clothed in a deerskin dress.

"Yes, Sarah and Briton have been very kind to me," I said, giving Sarah a grateful smile. "I got caught in the storm early this morning, and Briton offered me a ride."

Was it only this morning? I thought wildly. It felt much longer, but it was only mid-afternoon.

"But why would a young woman your age be travelling alone?" the oldest woman asked pointedly. "Especially for such a long way."

I took a deep breath, preparing myself for the hardest part of my story. It was always painful saying the words, but I knew I had to get used to it.

"My father was a Confederate Colonel, and when Atlanta surrendered to the Union, we left." My stomach curdled at the memory. "Union soldiers killed my parents outside the city. My little sister..."

I broke off, tears choking me as I thought of Leila. The women all looked at me in concern.

"Her soul is too troubled to speak," the oldest woman said firmly. "She's not ready for her story yet."

The other women nodded in agreement, but I stubbornly held up my hand. I had to continue. Saying it now would be just as painful as saying it later.

"No, I'm fine," I said, swallowing the tears and breathing through the pain in my chest. "My little sister and I ran into the woods and walked until we found an inn. The woman there kindly cared for us until a wealthy couple offered to adopt my sister. They took her with them, and I decided to go to New York. There might be more work up north."

I scoffed inwardly at the thought that it was *my* decision to go to New York. The women's eyes were wide with horror at my story, and many made sympathetic mumbles.

"Bless you, child," the oldest woman said gently. "You have a strong spirit to be so brave. So you're travelling to New York alone? Have you no other family?"

I shook my head, looking at the dirt floor beneath my moccasin-covered feet.

"It would be dangerous to look for them in Atlanta now," I muttered. The weight of memory was heavy, and I suddenly felt tired again.

"Have some more stew," Sarah offered. "It will help."

She didn't say in what way, but I accepted, acknowledging that having a warm meal worked wonders for rejuvenating energy. It gave me the courage to start asking questions instead.

"What is your name?" I asked the oldest woman, sensing that she was the leader of this group.

"I'm called Betsey," she said, but the curl of her lip told me she wasn't thrilled with it. "But my given name is Black Feather."

"Which do you prefer?" I asked, genuinely curious.

She smiled at the question, and I saw that one of her front teeth was missing.

"I'll always prefer Black Feather," she said softly, "but it's best if you call me Betsey."

I nodded, and the talking turned to more immediate concerns within the tribe. Apparently, a woman's husband had passed away a few days ago, and tonight they were performing a ceremonial dance in his honour. There was much to prepare, and since I was available, they put me to use quite quickly.

I spent the next few hours learning how to weave, pluck feathers, and grind corn. I also learned that although I was fairly skilled at domestic tasks, I severely lacked the coordination for basket weaving. The women were quite entertained by my efforts, but I wasn't offended. It was done in a friendly way. Despite feeling so out of place, I found the women's company comforting and fun. It had been a long time since I had socialised, and I found that I quite missed it. Although these brown-skinned, rustic women were far different from the hoop-skirted debutantes I was friends with back in Atlanta, the female camaraderie was the same. I felt a sharp jolt of realisation that I would never get a chance to wear my own red debutante dress or attend the ball my father would have thrown for me. A small lump formed in my throat. I had never thought much about life outside of my southern home. My circle had been small, consisting of a few school friends and neighbours.

Now, I was fascinated to learn about a culture and people I had heard only myths about. The conversation flowed naturally between us, and none of us seemed to mind being asked questions.

"We are many people from different tribes; The Saponi, Catawba, and Eno. We call ourselves Yesah, meaning 'the people,'" Sarah explained, responding to my question about where the Occaneechi people came from.

"Why did the tribes join together?" I asked, the idea of this intriguing.

"Survival, of course," one of the women replied. "By coming together, we could support one another.

Our traditions and customs are similar, so it was natural."

I pondered this as I scraped the pestle against the mortar filled with corn kernels. I admired their understanding and acceptance. I knew I couldn't say the same for the south. But then, there was a cultural difference, and that's where the true problem lay. It made me worry about how I was going to fit into the culture in the north. I couldn't help but voice this concern.

"Did any of you struggle to be part of another tribe?" I asked. "I'm a Confederate on my way to live in the north."

The women nodded sympathetically, understanding my worry. Betsey cocked her head and stared at me, thinking heavily. Her weaving fingers slowed as she weighed her response.

"There is always struggle with change," she finally said seriously. "The people here recognised they were different in some ways, but opened their minds to accept it. Perhaps that is your answer."

"Change has been our way of life for a long time now," Sarah agreed, nodding as she continued to pluck feathers. "We had to accept God as a replacement to the Creator. That was possibly the hardest of all."

The women all murmured in agreement. The sun started to set, sending a warm orange glow throughout the wigwam. I could hear children playing outside, laughing as they ran carefree through the village. Men were shouting to one another with orders and conversation as they busied themselves for the evening hunt. It was a peaceful community, and I could see why the different tribes had managed to come together.

"Do you believe in the Creator anymore?" I asked curiously. This seemed to shock some of the women, but others considered the question more seriously.

"I believe in both," Betsey declared, and some of the women gasped as if she had said something scandalous. Betsey cast a challenging eye at each of them. "Well, I do, and I'm not afraid to say so. I believe that God and the Creator work together, much like our tribes do. It creates harmony."

I smiled at her, grateful for her honest reply. She grinned and continued her work. Everyone stayed quiet for a time, focusing on their work and letting the seriousness of the conversation subside. I could tell that none of the women would argue with Betsey, whether they agreed with her or not. Before I knew it, the sun had set, and the men were back from the hunt.

"The moon should be up now," Sarah told everyone, and they gathered their work to leave. She turned to me. "We'll dance first, and then we'll feast in honour of the dead."

I stepped outside the wigwam with the other women, casting an eye at the moonlight gleaming off the wigwams. How had time passed so quickly? Sarah looked at the sky and smiled.

"The storm has passed. We can see the Wicawa nu^{n}ti," she said, pointing towards the moon. "This is good. Our dance for the dead is best if it's clear."

I didn't know why the moon should have anything to do with it except for giving enough light for the dancers to see by. It seemed strange to me that there should be dancing at all. I expected a solemn, respectful gathering with perhaps a few prayers. It only took the first unearthly cry to realise that I was wrong. The entire village was suddenly alive with a fevered current that ran from person to person. It was like a tide sweeping everyone up into the same frenzy of excitement and passion. The shrill, off-key cries of the dancers sent shivers up my spine, and I felt genuinely frightened. I had never heard such terrifying screams in my life. Sarah saw my face and grasped my arm as she pulled me towards a large circle where everyone was gathering around an enormous bonfire.

"This is a ceremonial dance," she explained over the beat of the drums and pipes. "Music and dancing are how we help the person's spirit rise to the ancestors."

I could only nod, struck speechless by the cacophony of sights and sounds around us. It was all too foreign for me to process. The dancers were dressed in full deerskin clothing, covered with ornamental beads, tassels, and feathers. Their outfits were ornate and eye-catching, purposely designed to attract attention. They danced in two-beat steps and twirled around the fire, raising their hands rhythmically to the strong beat of the music, their cries echoing throughout the village. It was primitive and intimidating, but at the same time, I felt the sense of excitement that rippled through the crowd. This wasn't simply for show; this was a celebration. One of the dancers came close to us, and I recognised Briton. He looked completely different in the moonlight and full Indian dress. I thought he looked more natural.

"So you have kept some of your customs," I said to Sarah as we sat down at the edge of the circle. "Where does God come into this?"

I gestured around us, and Sarah chuckled, her body swaying in rhythm to the music.

"I suppose Betsey was right," she admitted. "Believing in God doesn't mean we have to stop practising our traditions. I suppose we now have two Creators to pray to, which can only be good. We are protected by both."

Protected by both. Was that how it was for me? I believed in God, but now I also had Spirits guiding me. Were they like the Creator for the Occaneechi? It was a relief to think that, like them, I could believe in both, and be protected and guided by both. Perhaps Betsey was right, and they worked together. I glanced over at Sarah and wondered if I should tell her about the Spirits. Certainly, people who danced under the moon to guide a person's spirit to the ancestors wouldn't think my Spirits were anything alarming. Still, a part of me hesitated, not quite sure how to tell her about them. I focused instead on the dancers and noticed how they swooped so low that the fringes on their jackets, leggings, and dresses would touch the ground. After a while, it became obvious that this was done on purpose, and I wondered why.

"When the fringe touches the ground, it honours the ancestors," Sarah explained when I asked. "The more we honour them, the more pleased they are and will accept the spirit."

I nodded, feeling my heart beat with the powerful drums around us. The singing was ear-shattering and hard to focus on, but the rhythm of the drums sent a pulse through me. In these circumstances, I could believe in almost anything. In a sudden moment of impulse, I decided to share my secret.

"I'm being guided by Spirits," I confessed, and Sarah's head whipped round, her eyes wide with shock. "But I don't know what they are."

I gave a brief description of how they came to me, and as I explained, Sarah's face transitioned from shock to wariness, then to thoughtfulness. After a few moments of pensive thought, she gave my arm a comforting squeeze.

"They are guiding you, which is good," she said firmly. "Perhaps they are your ancestors."

"My ancestors," I repeated dubiously, but I didn't have any better ideas. "Why would my ancestors care where I go?"

Sarah smiled. "Our ancestors always care about us," she said softly. "We are connected to them. Perhaps even God is sending your ancestors to you. It's difficult to say, but you are being protected, and that is good."

She gave a definitive shrug, which seemed to say as long as these Spirits were good and not evil, I shouldn't question too much where they came from. I wished I could have her faith, but it confused me.

I was becoming used to the music and even the singing. I began to sway with Sarah, who raised her arms towards the fire and joined the singing. As the cries of the dancers and the beat of the drums radiated through me, I found myself wondering why I doubted Sarah's opinion. Perhaps God *had* decided to use my ancestors to guide me. Hadn't the pastor always said He worked in mysterious ways? It was not for me to question how The Almighty wanted to work. It also made me feel better to know that perhaps the Spirits were connected to Him the same way Betsey felt her Creator was. As Sarah had implied, it didn't matter in the end. I was being protected.

I cleared my mind of everything except my surroundings; the heat of the fire, the scent of roasted meat and body odour, and the bright colours of the dancer's dresses. It culminated into a pulsating body of light, colour, and sound. Overseeing all of it was the solemn silence of the harvest moon.

Chapter Eight

It took another day of rest and food to help me fully recover. Soon, my blisters were almost healed, and my energy revived. My Spirits said to me that it was time to leave. Sarah and Briton seemed sorry to see me go as they helped me pack. With a critical glance at my heavy luggage case, Briton had given a disapproving grunt and replaced it with a light deerskin rucksack with tassels. Attached to it were long, black straps with red and white beads that I could wrap over my neck and across my shoulders to carry on my back.

"This will be much lighter to carry," he explained as he showed me how to wear it. "It can also carry just as much, if not more."

The rucksack was surprisingly light and I knew I wouldn't miss my clunky luggage case for a moment. My clothes had dried and could be worn again, apart from the threadbare shawl and boots. Sarah replaced it with a cosy animal hide shawl lined with soft grey rabbit fur. She gently placed this over my shoulders, her light brown eyes warmly gazing into mine.

"Nothing is warmer than fur," she stated firmly, "and nothing is better for long travel than moccasins."

She pointed to my feet which still wore the moccasins she had given me. I wasn't going to argue with her. They were pliable and soft, yet sturdy. I felt as if I could walk in them all day, and they weren't as heavy as my boots either. Briton, Sarah, and the tribe had also pooled together some money to give me for my travels.

"Thank you, both of you," I said, choking up at their kindness. "I truly don't know what I would have done without you."

We stood outside the wigwams near the path that would lead out of Little Texas and back onto the main road. It was morning, giving me a fresh start for a day's travelling. I was heading for Philadelphia, but it would take me six days, according to Briton and the other tribesmen, to make it through Virginia and into Pennsylvania. Betsey and the other women had come earlier that morning, bearing food and well-wishes for my travels.

"Stay brave," Betsey had said firmly, squeezing my shoulder with her strong, basket-weaving fingers. "Always remember, to adapt is to survive."

She had raised her eyebrows pointedly at this, and I took her meaning well. She knew I was a Confederate heading into enemy territory. It was going to take more than just bravery to conquer that challenge.

I remembered her words as I said my farewells to Sarah and Briton. The rest of the village watched in the distance, everyone curious to witness me leaving. I turned my gaze back to Sarah.

"I'll think of you all during my travels," I promised, turning to each of them. "For your kindness, hospitality, and acceptance. I have learned so much from you."

Sarah's eyes lit up with appreciation, and she hugged me gently. Briton grinned and gave a short nod.

"It's been wonderful knowing you, Ora," Sarah said softly. "Go with your Spirits and be safe."

I shifted the rucksack higher onto my shoulders, making sure the rabbit-fur shawl was safely tucked underneath the straps. I flexed my toes in the soft moccasins, enjoying the airy feel of them. As I walked out of the village, I felt as if I had left an old part of me behind. I was stripped of some of my old belongings and clothing, but felt refreshed and stronger with the new replacements.

"Adapt indeed," I muttered to myself as I turned onto the main road.

I was on my way, feeling much more prepared for whatever I faced. Meeting the Occaneechi had taught me that what I didn't know or understand, I could learn and possibly even be better off for it.

It was a crisp autumn day with a slight breeze, though thankfully, it was dry. The sun was out, but it was only for show, and I was grateful to be dressed warmly. It felt strange being on my own again after nearly two full days of having company. The silence along the road seemed almost ominous, and I hummed to myself to break it. It surprised me how quickly I missed the constant chatter of the I^{n}ya and the bustling activity of the I^{n}ye^n preparing for their hunts. I smiled to myself as I thought of the women and men in the Siouan language. I hadn't grasped much of it, but what I had stuck with me.

Alone with only my thoughts, I could plan once more. I had a rough idea of where I was heading, though I knew I would have to get directions along the way. This was never very difficult, provided someone at the inn was knowledgeable and willing to share information for nothing. I frowned as I remembered a few who had wanted more than a thank you for their troubles, but I was always lucky to have someone come to my aide. Luck or blessed by the Spirits, I wasn't too sure.

Towards evening time, I had run out of tunes to hum and was forced to listen to the rustling leaves and wind for company. It was times like these that I wished the Spirits could talk with me. Not just give me orders or guidance, but chat with me as if they were a friend.

You're losing it, Ora, I thought ruefully, stopping to take a sip from the canteen Briton had placed in my rucksack. *Now you're so desperate you'll talk to entities in thin air*!

The water cleared my muddled head, and I breathed the fresh air deeply. Hours of nothing but silence aside from mindless humming had put my brain to sleep, but the cold, sharp tang of the water roused me again. The sun was resting on the treetops, the red glow of evening beginning to match the autumn hues. My stomach grumbled as if on cue to remind me that it was nearing dinnertime. I looked down at it, gave it a pat, and nodded.

"Let's hope there's an inn nearby," I told my stomach, and then chuckled. I really was losing my mind.

Over several days of travelling, I learned how to tell time from the sun and my stomach. They were surprising companions, often following the same schedule. It wasn't something I had ever noticed before, and it made me think about how one of the Occaneechi women had mentioned our bodies working along with nature. I mused over this when I heard the sound of wagons. I glanced behind me then realised that the sound was ahead, along with far-off voices. Only an inn could attract that many voices and wagons, and I quickened my steps, my moccasin-covered feet skimming lightly over the stones in the dirt. It occurred to me as I neared closer that it could be a group of soldiers, and I quickly scanned the forest around me to see if there was somewhere to hide. The trees were more sparse, having been cut away to make the road wider and didn't offer any hiding place, but fortunately, I caught sight of the inn.

I slowed down, heaving a grateful sigh. So far, my luck had held out in finding inns as long as I stayed on the main road. Some were further apart than others, but I had always managed to find one eventually. This one seemed sizeable to my relief, which meant it most likely had available accommodation. Although, it was also busy. I pursed my lips with consternation as I stepped up to the door, looking at the rows of wagons and horses heading for the livery in the back. Boisterous shouts and loud voices also told me that it was predominantly men occupying it at the moment.

Wait outside, the Spirits' voice chimed in my ear.

I obeyed, knowing better than to second-guess them. I stepped away from the door and moved over to the left. Not a second later, a man's body was thrown out of the door and onto the dirt. Had I hesitated a second longer, he would have hit me. I gasped and stared at the man shadowing the doorway who had catapulted his acquaintance. He turned to me, his eyes bloodshot with drink and sneered crudely.

"What're you staring at, Injun girl?" he hissed, his words slurring as he swayed.

I held my head high and shook my head.

"Nothing at all," I replied firmly, refusing to look over at the groaning man on the ground. "I was just passing by."

I waited for the drunken man to turn his attention back on his friend before moving. My heart was pounding so hard that I felt light-headed. Fortunately, he seemed too focused on his adversary to care about what I was doing. I took the chance and risked crossing the front of the inn, having to sidestep the fallen man to do so. I decided to go to the livery, since it seemed the only quiet place and safe away from the chaos at the inn. As I started towards it, I heard the drunken man call out to me.

"Come over here, Injun!" he called, his thick voice rough with desire. "I wasn't done talking with you!"

I lightly hopped behind one of the wagons, shielding myself from his view.

"Oh, but I'm done talking with you," I muttered to myself.

It would be dark soon, so continuing on wasn't an option. It would be too dangerous to be on the road in the pitch-black where I couldn't see and possibly freeze to death. No, I had to stay at this inn, but unfortunately, it seemed too dangerous to enter. I heard the groaning man rise to his feet. I peeked past the wagon to see if the men were gone. The groaning man was staggering back to the door, but I couldn't see where the drunken man was. Fear snaked its way up my spine, and I had that innate sense of being watched.

I crouched down, seeing if I could hide underneath a wagon. When I did, I saw two boots on the other side.

"There you are, honey," his voice growled, and the boots moved to come around the wagon. "You need company tonight."

I watched him stride around the wagon with a leering grin on his bearded face. Desperately, I searched for anything to hit him with or anywhere to hide. Unfortunately, the wagons were crowded close together and were all empty.

Not one person brought belongings? I thought wildly.

I saw the entrance to the livery and raced for it. I almost reached the entrance when I was pulled back by rough hands on my waist. A primitive scream built in my throat, and as I turned around, I let it go into his face.

"You'll let me go!" I ordered, fear and anger combating one another. I couldn't decide if I wanted to run or kill him.

He laughed boisterously, his whiskey-soured breath washing my face and making me gag.

"You won't be orderin' me," he snapped, his hands clutching my arms as I struggled. "Not a nice little plump hen like you."

I could hear the lust in his voice and panicked. He had knocked the rucksack and shawl off my back and was finding his way up my skirts. I kicked at him, and he smacked me hard.

"Mind yer manners now," he spat.

My head swam as tears blurred my vision. I had never been hit in my life. All I could think of was to scream and pray.

Help me! I pleaded, not knowing if it was to God, the Spirits, or both. I'd take anyone at this point, even the devil himself if he'd get this monster off of me.

He had me on the ground now, my arms pinned behind my head, and I feebly tried to kick him, but my heavy skirts prevented me. Growling with frustration, I spat in his face. He reared back in surprise, roaring with anger, and raised his fist.

"Ye little bit..." He was cut off by a sharp crack against his head.

His eyes rolled back, and his jaw went slack. He fell to the side, and I gasped for air. My arms were sore and stiff, and I stretched them self-consciously as I stared wide-eyed at the shadowed figure standing before me. The lamp he had placed on the ground outlined his body as he extended a hand to help me up.

"Y'all right?" he asked, deep worry in his voice. "I heard you screamin' and came out fast as I could."

I took his offered hand, noting that it was rough with calluses and warm. Shakily, I stood up and gingerly stepped to the side to avoid the still figure of the drunken man. Brushing myself off, I watched him to be sure he was indeed passed out cold. Seeing that he was, I looked up at my saviour and felt surprised to see an onyx-black face staring back at me, his white eyes pronounced in the dusk. I shook off the surprise and smiled as politely as I could under the circumstances.

"Thank you," I said. My voice was slightly hoarse from screaming. "What did you hit him with?"

The man seemed astonished at the question.

"Oh, this here, ma'am," he said, holding up a pitchfork. "I thought stabbing him would get blood on you, so I just gave him a good wallop across the head."

I raised my eyebrows and smiled.

"Thanks for your concern," I grinned. "Who are you?"

We had stepped away from the drunken man to the livery yard entrance. I was still shaking, but grateful.

"My name's Abner," the stableman said, nodding politely. "I work here in the livery."

"Ora," I replied graciously, taking a deep breath as I collected my thoughts. "I was hoping to stay at this inn tonight, but it seems quite dangerous."

Abner nodded apologetically, rolling his lips as if they were dry.

"Sorry about that," he said, giving a hopeless shrug towards the inn. "A rowdy group of highwaymen came in about an hour ago, raisin' the roof enough to wake the dead. My boss normally don't abide by such groups, but they paid up straight off, so he let them stay."

He raised a finger for me to wait a moment, and quickly gathered up my rabbit fur shawl and rucksack.

"These yours?" he asked quizzically.

"Yes, thank you," I said, giving him a gracious smile. "I appreciate your saving me. Now I just don't know what to do."

Abner watched me, his face thoughtful. I couldn't imagine what he was thinking, but his staring made me uncomfortable. I didn't mind black people as a rule, but having been brought up by well-mannered slaves, it was hard not to snap at him, even knowing he was a free man.

"Yes?" I finally asked, my tone slightly sharp.

"Where you from?" Abner asked gravely. "You've a deep accent from the south, but I've never seen a southern woman dressed up like an Injun."

"Atlanta," I replied shortly. "I found friends with the Occaneechi who gave me these. I'm travelling to New York City."

Abner's mouth dropped open before he caught himself. Staring at me with surprise, he pursed his lips tightly.

"Confederate?" he asked warily.

I hesitated, not quite sure what I was anymore. I didn't feel like the same girl who had left Atlanta. A lot had happened since then. My time with the Occaneechi had opened my eyes to see people differently from what I had believed. I looked at Abner thoughtfully, seeing him in a different light as well. At one point, he would have been nothing but the black help, here to tend to my needs and nothing more. I knew and accepted this about myself. It had been my culture. But now I saw him as the Occaneechi might see him, as they had seen me. A man who had helped to save a girl from trouble. He was a person, the same as me.

"I was Confederate," I replied carefully, looking him straight in the eye, "but times are changing for me too."

He raised his brows at this and nodded. He knew what I meant. He was free now, and I was moving north from the south. I gave a tiny grin as Betsey's words floated through my mind. *Adapt to survive.*

"In that case, I think it's best if you stay in the barn tonight," he offered kindly. "It's not the most comfortable, but it's safe, dry, and private."

I nearly laughed at this recitation of Briton's description of a wigwam, but held it in, not wanting to confuse Abner.

"That would be most kind," I said happily.

I lifted the rucksack and shawl onto my shoulders and pointed at the drunken man still lying on the ground.

"What do we do with him?" I asked gravely.

Abner frowned. "*We* do nothing," he said shortly. "I'll tell my boss, and he'll sort him out."

I agreed with this, relieved not to have any part in it. All I wanted at the moment was to sit down, eat, and then sleep. My adrenaline from earlier was dissipating, leaving me bone-tired. I followed Abner to the barn. He opened the door, and a scented wave of hay, manure, and horse hair hit me full in the face. I wrinkled my nose but followed willingly as Abner led me up a rickety set of wooden stairs to a hay loft.

"This will have to do, ma'am," he said politely. "I'll talk to my boss about getting some food to you."

He began heading down the stairs again, turning back with a friendly grin.

"And if you don't mind, I'd like to hear your story."

He disappeared before he could see me roll my eyes. I plopped down into the hay and groaned. Why did everyone want to hear my story? I also wasn't sure what Abner would make of it, considering that my father had been a Confederate Colonel. I puzzled over how much to tell him as I shifted the straw around to create a nest for myself. The straw was stiff and poked me everywhere, but I was inside and safe.

Thank you, Spirits, I thought before shutting my eyes to rest.

I was a little apprehensive about explaining to Abner everything that had happened to me. After all, how much empathy could he have for a girl with a background like mine?

Chapter Nine

Nothing but the scratching of my fork on the tin plate could be heard for a while after I finished telling Abner my story. It hadn't taken long, being fairly straightforward, but the details seemed to leave the man pensive and quiet. He leaned back against a hay bale, twirling a piece of straw between his teeth. Normally I would have been offended by his casual manner with me, considering it highly disrespectful, but in these circumstances I didn't mind. We were in a barn, with me hardly being in a respectable state myself. I glanced at the dirty, brown patches on my arms, dusty from travelling. We shared the common bond of being outcasts, even if it was only for a moment. I found Abner to be surprisingly enjoyable company and easy to talk to. He was mild-mannered, direct, and had a kind personality that warmed me to him.

"Well, I'll be," he whistled through his teeth, shaking his head slowly. "I've heard some mighty strange tales lately, what with the war and all, but that trumps all of them."

I shrugged noncommittally, not caring if my story was more entertaining than others. As usual, I had left out the Spirits part and had no intention of mentioning them. Setting my empty plate aside, I smoothed my skirts, realising how crumpled they were. I suddenly felt like a little girl again, playing a game, like when I had stepped into the wigwam. Nothing seemed real to me. Sitting in this hay loft with a black man felt as foreign to me as sitting with the Occaneechi. It suddenly occurred to me that I might never be seen as a respectable woman again. I was a rogue and an orphan with no place to call a proper home. I felt the tears rising, and I swallowed before they could break through.

"How far until I reach Virginia?" I asked, deciding to direct my attention on practical matters.

Abner laughed gleefully, smacking a hand on his homespun trousers.

"You're in Virginia!" he crowed, and I widened my eyes. "Not sure where the border is exactly, but you're in Lynchburg at the moment. Another day's walk will bring you to Charlottesville."

My heart lightened at the thought of a proper town. I was still in Confederate territory, although I knew the lines would start to blur. The west of the state had joined the Union, so I wasn't sure how many Union soldiers I could potentially run into.

"I warn you, though," Abner continued, frowning thoughtfully, "Charlottesville will be the last city you'll come to before Baltimore, which is in Maryland. You might have trouble finding inns along that way."

I nodded, taking his warning seriously, though not knowing what I could really do about it.

"I'll manage," I said firmly, smiling to soften my tone. I was worried, but I didn't want Abner to know it.

Maryland would be my last safe haven before reaching the north. I had heard mixed news regarding the state's side of the war. I knew they had never officially seceded from the Union but still kept slaves, and many Marylanders fought on the Confederate side. But there were Union soldiers there as well, so I knew I had to tread carefully, depending on who I was speaking to. Some would welcome my broad Georgian accent, and some might not.

"Do you happen to know how far it is from Charlottesville to Baltimore?" I asked, hoping that Abner might know since he seemed to be a wealth of information.

He cocked his head, thinking for a moment.

"It's around a two-day walk, I suspect," he mused, rubbing his lips together again. "I wouldn't think more from what I hear from travelling folk."

Abner shrugged and gave an apologetic smile before standing up and brushing hay from his backside. "Unfortunately, that's as much as I know, but no doubt folk will give you more answers when you reach Charlottesville. When you leavin'?"

"At first light," I said, my heart thumping nervously at the thought of being alone on the road again. I desperately hoped that drunken fool wouldn't be around.

Abner saw the concern on my face and gave me a reassuring pat on the arm. I nearly jumped at his touch but stopped myself.

"Don't you worry none about that man," he said firmly, his tone so serious I believed him. "My boss will have already taken care of him."

This sounded distinctly ominous, but I didn't interrogate further. As long as Abner thought I was safe, I felt I should trust him. He picked up his lantern, leaving a second one with me, along with a stern warning not to let it break or else the whole barn would catch fire. This terrified me, and I knew I would blow out the candle the minute he left.

"Thank you, Abner," I said to him quickly as he started to descend down the rickety stairs. "It's been nice meeting you."

He flashed me a bright grin, knowing full well that a girl from my background wouldn't be used to spending time with black people. He tipped his head towards me.

"It's been nice meetin' you too," he replied warmly. "I'll come at first light to make sure you've woken up and give you some breakfast."

I watched him leave, listening to the comforting sounds of the horses chewing their hay and rustling in the straw. Calm horses meant there wasn't anyone prowling around the barn. If anyone came in, I would know it by their alerting snorts or questioning nickers. It was warmer in the hay loft than I had expected, and I supposed it was due to the body heat of the animals beneath me. Abner had brought me a coarse wool blanket with my dinner. I wrapped this around me gratefully, finding a cosy place on the hay to lay my head, and blew out the candle, letting the darkness envelop me.

To my relief, but not surprise, Abner was true to his word and greeted me at first light. Dawn was just breaking, allowing enough light to peek through the barn slats for me to see my breakfast. The morning air was chilly, and I wrapped the blanket tighter around my shoulders.

"Take it with you," he offered. "I can get another."

"Are you sure?" I asked, frowning. I didn't want to take his only blanket. "I have my shawl."

Abner waved his hand dismissively.

"It's mine to give," he said firmly.

I hesitated, unsure of how easy it would be for him to obtain another one, but I didn't want to insult him. From his tone, I could tell the freedom to own anything was a matter of pride for a freed black man; I wasn't about to throw that back in his face.

"Thank you," I said gratefully. "What do I owe for the lodging and food?"

He set down a tin plate with my breakfast, and I was happy to see buttered grits with a lightly fried egg.

"My boss said since your lodging was in the barn, he'd only charge you one dollar for the food," Abner explained.

This sounded reasonable, and I happily paid. As I ate, Abner went about his work tending to the horses and shovelling dirty straw and manure outside. It was remarkably cosy sitting in the hay warmed by my body, and I felt like one of the sparrows in the rafters sitting in their nests, watching the activity below. I could have perched there all day, but I knew that time was passing, and a day's travel lay before me.

Once I was packed, the new woollen blanket tucked away with my other belongings, I gave Abner a fond farewell and started off again, relieved to see no sign of the drunken man. I shifted my rucksack on my shoulders and began to hum.

To my profound relief, the day's walk to Charlottesville was completely uneventful. Though I was as lonely as ever, I was happy that lodging was easy to come by, with an abundant number of hotels in the city, along with several factories, banks, and even six print shops for newspapers. However, the city's interest ended there, since the remainder of it felt like a small village made up of simple frame houses. I chose the cheapest and safest accommodation I could, and after a good night's sleep, I headed out the next morning for Baltimore. According to the hotel owner, Abner had been correct in assuming it was a two-days walk.

That was my only concern as I left Charlottesville, as I knew it would likely be a roadside inn I would have to stay in that night. I was a little more hesitant of them now after my experience with the drunken man in Lynchburg, but I knew it was either risk an inn or sleep outside.

By the time the sun set, I decided to risk the inn. After all, for the majority of my journey, I had experienced very few issues with them. The Spirits seemed happy enough with the decision, and I spent a quiet night as one of the sole lodgers in the establishment. In the morning, the elderly man running the inn told me that I was in Alexandria, near the border of Maryland, and a day's walk away from Baltimore. He seemed to accept that I was travelling to New York without too much enquiry and wished me well. As I prepared to leave, I ran my fingers over the soles of the moccasins. They were holding strong, as Sarah had told me, but my feet were beginning to ache. I wished I could afford to stay another night, since this inn was the quietest I had been to, but money was tight. I didn't know if another windfall of generosity would come my way.

Despite my weary legs and sore feet, I made surprisingly good time and arrived in Baltimore during nightfall. The walk had taken a bit longer since the roads were becoming more mountainous, but my travelling had strengthened my endurance, and I could continue on despite the hilly terrain. I had been worried about meeting Union soldiers and encountering any fighting around this time. To my surprise, it was relatively quiet on the roads with nothing more than the usual travellers. I approached a respectable inn and enquired about this to the innkeeper, Maggie, as I paid for a night's lodging.

"The fighting has mostly gone down south now," Maggie told me brusquely, raising an inquisitive brow at my southern accent. "You're looking for peace; you're heading in the right direction."

This sounded promising and I thanked her, turning away before that inquisitive brow could evolve into questions. I was in Maryland now, and I knew that the further north I went, the more my accent would spark questions. Although I hardly appeared to be a typical southern lady anymore, I was obviously not from the north.

My room at Maggie's was sparse but large, and it had a bed with a down comforter that I longed for. However, before I settled, I decided to count how much money I had left. I did this periodically, not wanting to lose track. A part of me was hoping I might have enough to spare for a stagecoach to Philadelphia, the next largest city. I knew this would be an unnecessary splurge, but my throbbing feet pleaded for respite.

As I counted the coins, I weighed the risk of spending what would be around two dollars. That was a night's food and lodging, so a heavy consideration when I didn't know how much further I had. My eyelids drooped, and the room swam as exhaustion consumed me. I would have to look into it more tomorrow.

The next morning my enquiries were easily answered. A stagecoach would be leaving in two hours if I was interested. I also learned that I was four days from New York City. This lightened my spirits immensely. Four days didn't sound long at all, and I was hopeful that I would find employment quickly once I got there.

"One thing to consider," Maggie said as she placed my breakfast of doughnuts and tea in front of me, "is that the stagecoach will be a whole lot safer than walking."

I had confided my concerns to her when I asked about the stagecoach. She quickly learned that I was travelling alone and had immediately been warmer towards me.

"I can't deny that's true," I agreed, taking a bite of scrumptious doughnut. "Thank you for your concern."

She smiled and patted my arm before walking away to help someone else. The stagecoach would take a day and a half. It was safer and faster, but there was a price for convenience, and I hoped I could afford it. The thrifty part of me was losing the inner battle. The temptation of safety and comfort was simply too strong to resist. Although it would leave me with only enough money for one night's lodging, I decided to risk it. After all, I had worked for lodging in other inns. Perhaps I'd find one who would be willing to do it again.

Two hours later, my thrifty side was well and truly quieted as I climbed into the stagecoach. I was tightly squeezed between a woman and the stagecoach window but happy not to be travelling under my own power anymore. I ignored the baffled looks the drivers gave my rucksack as they threw it on top of the stagecoach with the other luggage cases. The other passengers, two men and a woman, gave me quizzical stares. I simply stared out the window. I didn't care what they thought about my moccasins or rucksack. All I cared about was the city rolling by me.

I hadn't been in a carriage since leaving Atlanta with my parents, and the memory made me bite my lip to keep from crying. I hadn't expected the motion of the stagecoach to bring back our family carriage so poignantly. Images flashed before me of our former slaves standing in line, waving to us, Phibe's crying face, our solid white house, and little Leila curled next to me as Mama told me her story. An involuntary painful gasp escaped me, making the woman next to me jump and look at me in alarm. I smiled at her as reassuringly as I could before I turned back to the window, pressing the cold glass against my face to stop the tears from falling.

"I will not cry," I whispered, ordering myself to keep it together.

I could feel the woman turn towards me as I spoke, but I ignored her. The hard lump in my throat was too large to talk, and I knew I would cry if I had to explain my situation. I hadn't felt anything familiar since I'd left Winnie. Being in a stagecoach again was almost overwhelming, and it made me more emotional than I was prepared for. As the miles went by, I gathered myself back together again. *Memories must stay locked away in the past,* I told myself firmly. *Only the future matters now.* I was one city away from reaching the place my Spirits beckoned me to. The future was nearly here, and I felt a sense of dread and excitement. Once I was in New York City, my travels would be over, and real life would have to be built once more. But first, I had to survive Philadelphia.

Chapter Ten

I woke up with a start and painful stiffness in my neck when the stagecoach lumbered to a sudden stop. The drivers' voices bellowed down to us, announcing our arrival in Philadelphia. The other passengers had also been dozing, and we all slowly stirred. I squinted out the window with heavy, sleep-filled eyes at the dismal sky with low grey clouds outlined by a struggling afternoon sun. The coach began shifting as the other passengers descended, and I shook myself awake to follow suit. My rucksack was hastily dropped into my arms the second my foot touched the cobblestone road.

"G'day, ma'am," the driver said quickly before his head disappeared on top of the stagecoach.

I nodded, not bothering to reply. It wasn't expected anyway. My head felt stuffed with cotton, and my eyes like sandpaper. Although travelling by stagecoach had been faster and safer, it didn't allow a full night's rest, and I knew the rest of the day would be agony. I needed to find a place to sit down, clear my foggy state, and make a plan. I judged it to be late afternoon, and the streets were filled with people. The crowds made it easy to disappear since everyone was too busy and in a hurry to notice a lone girl walking through them.

The stagecoach had dropped us near a wooden footpath on the corner of two streets. I glanced down both, trying to decide which way seemed best. One street continued over a small bridge, and the other was lined with shop fronts. I chose the latter, figuring where there were shops, there could be hotels. My nervousness about being in the north settled as I realised I wasn't attracting attention.

Until I open my mouth, I thought ruefully.

As long as I stayed quiet, I would be safe enough. The real test would be when I had to find accommodation. My legs felt unsteady after sitting for so many hours, reminding me of when sailors came off the ships and talked about finding their land legs again. As I drifted up the street, glancing at each shop front in a dreamlike state, I remembered an old sea captain who had been a friend of my father's. He had been invited for dinner a few years ago, and he and Papa had enjoyed a marvellous time recalling war stories and military jargon. I could vividly imagine our elegant dining room and the savoury smell of the roast pork dinner Phibe brought in with boiled corn and sweet potatoes.

My stomach rumbled suddenly, jarring me back to the reality of the cold, grey streets around me. I realised that I was still half-asleep and groggy. I reached into my rucksack for the canteen that I prayed still had water in it. It did, although only a little. I drank what was left and pinched my cheeks to sharpen my focus. The footpaths were so full that the crowds overflowed onto the busy street filled with coaches, light traps, and supply wagons.

I pushed through the people as politely as I could, though this was difficult considering that no one was polite back. I wasn't used to this kind of atmosphere and missed the slow southern pace of Atlanta. No one was ever in a hurry down south, though one could argue that it was due to the oppressive heat. It was hard to move fast when the humidity was heavy.

A bitter wind whipped through my shawl, and I shivered. Perhaps this was why everyone in Philadelphia was in a rush. It was to escape the blasted cold! I had never felt such an arctic chill before and quickened my pace. The street was long and winding, and it must have taken me a good hour before I finally reached a hotel at the end of it. My cheeks flushed with the cold and my brisk pace. I pushed open the door and walked in, trembling from head to toe with exhaustion.

"What can I do for you, ma'am?" asked the hotel clerk.

"I'd like a room for tonight, please," I replied, trying to curb my southern accent as best I could. Unfortunately, it didn't work.

The clerk's thin eyebrows rose pointedly, and her lips pursed as she regarded me with an aloof expression.

"Southern, are you?" she snapped, and my heart sank.

"Yes, I'm on my way to New York," I said, keeping my tone polite but feeling miffed at her immediate presumption of who I was.

"We don't take kindly to Confederates in this establishment," she said, sneering down at me as if I was an insect that had crawled in. "Perhaps you'd be best to find accommodation elsewhere."

An arguing retort rose in my throat, but I forcibly swallowed it as I battled with shock. I reminded myself that I had been prepared for this, or at least I thought I had, but experiencing it in real life was like a slap in the face. Over the weeks I'd been travelling, the war had always been a presence in one way or another, seeing soldiers on the road or in the taverns, and hearing people talk about it. Still, since my parents' deaths, I had never felt immediately affected by it throughout my journey. Now, the war was shoved rudely back into my life, and the same angry bubble of resentment I had felt in Atlanta when we had escaped bubbled under my calm demeanour.

I eyed the clerk steadily, staring straight into her solemn blue eyes until she shifted nervously. I didn't know what my face looked like exactly, but I had a good idea from the clerk's uneasy expression. A part of me knew that the war wasn't her fault any more than it was mine, but that Yankee attitude towards Confederates was why my family was gone, and this was hard for me to forget so easily.

"I don't take kindly to rude Yankees," I said calmly, turning my lips up into a smile that was just this side of polite, "but I wouldn't turn you onto the streets if the roles were switched. I suppose that's the difference between northern and southern hospitality."

I lifted my head high, gave her a pointed look, and turned briskly, my skirts swishing smartly around my legs as I strode out the door with a back straight enough to make Papa proud. I was not accustomed to being insulted, and it took me a few moments to quiet my sizzling anger long enough for me to think. I had a problem now. I highly doubted this was the only hotel that would react this way to a southerner. As the clerk had so politely reminded me, we were in a war after all.

"Thunderation," I cursed under my breath, exhaling a white puff of cold air.

It was far too chilly here to even consider sleeping on the streets. Finding accommodation was imperative, so I simply had to keep trying. For the next two hours, I stubbornly tried every hotel I came across as I explored the city, trying to hide my accent. Unfortunately, these attempts failed, and each hotel was just as stubborn about not letting me stay. When the grey streets turned darker, I began to get genuinely worried. I was getting so desperate that I begged the clerk at the next hotel.

"Hmm, I hate seeing a girl on these streets alone," he mused, tapping his lips with a thick forefinger, "even if you are a Confederate, albeit an odd one."

He glanced ruefully at my moccasins, rabbit shawl, and rucksack. I waited, hardly daring to hope that someone here would be kind. After being treated like this, I was deathly afraid of what would happen to me in New York. What were the Spirits thinking? The clerk's voice snapped me back from my musing.

"You won't have luck with the hotels," he informed me firmly, "so don't bother to continue trying. However, there's an establishment not too far from here that takes in freed slaves and outcasts. It's rough, but they won't turn you away."

I felt the blood drain from my face. This place sounded worse than the inn with the highwaymen in Lynchburg. Had it not been for Abner, I wouldn't have survived it. I mumbled my thanks, and he quickly gave me directions, the relief on his face evident that he was glad to be rid of me.

He probably thinks he did a good deed today, I thought bitterly as I stepped back outside into the chilly wind.

With no other options, I knew I had to risk this rough establishment. I would have walked slower since I wasn't in any hurry. However, whether I liked it or not, the night was fast approaching, along with the ruffians that typically accompanied it in a busy city. I turned down the directed street, keeping a fast pace and ignoring the occasional catcalls from the street urchins that lined the narrow alleyways. My heart thudded with fear as I finally approached the ramshackle inn that the clerk had mentioned. It was a seedy-looking place. The front looked like it had been beautiful at one point, with elegant woodwork and stained glass windowpanes, but it had weathered with age and now sagged, dull and lifeless. The stained glass was chipped, the woodwork broken, and the vibrant paint peeled away. A crowd of black men lounged casually at the front, smoking cigars and eyeing me with cautious suspicion. I hardly looked menacing, but I was white, and I knew that was enough.

I walked inside, hardly daring to hope for an improvement. There wasn't. The furniture was as tired and faded as the rest of the place. In fact, the whole atmosphere was dismal, tainted with an air of desperation. The few patrons I saw were a sorry sort, looking lost and worried. I realised with shock that I must look exactly like them. I stepped up to the clerk, at least not worried about being turned away this time. To my surprise, the clerk was a black woman, small-boned and short, with a determined air about her. She stared at me nonplussed, casting an interested eye over my unusual attire.

"How long do you need?" she asked abruptly, not bothering with courtesies. I couldn't decide at first whether I welcomed this or not. I was tired, impatient at being shut out all afternoon, and not in the mood for niceties. I decided it suited me fine.

"Only one night," I said shortly, looking around me with concern. More people were trickling in from outside, and from the corner of my eye, I could see they were black.

"Fifty cents then," she said, and I quickly gave it to her. She handed me a room key and pointed up the stairs. "First door on the left. If it doesn't open, give it a kick."

I nodded, but my stomach spoke up with an alarming growl. The black woman's interested gaze dropped quickly to my grumbling stomach and then rose to my face.

"We have a kitchen here too if you need supper," she remarked, her tone still indifferent but softer now. "Just sit at a table. It'll be a dollar."

I smiled gratefully, paid with the little money I had left, and trudged over to one of the wooden tables. The wood was chipped and filled with ring marks from wet glasses, but I didn't care. I was sitting down at last, and I was going to eat. The world seemed almost surreal as I watched the other patrons saunter in and out of the hotel. My head was nearly spinning with exhaustion and nerves, but I waited for food; my stomach wouldn't let me sleep otherwise. Before long, a little black girl came to the table, wearing a one-piece cotton frock that hung loosely on her. My heart squeezed as I looked into her young face. She couldn't have been more than six years old.

"You want supper, ma'am?" she asked timidly, her brown eyes as wide as a newborn fawn's as she stared at me. She was obviously nervous of me since I was a white woman. I smiled as encouragingly as I could and nodded.

"Yes, please, that would be wonderful," I said softly, trying not to scare her. "What's your name?" "Priscilla," she said, swallowing at being asked a question. With a short nod, she turned and left.

I noticed the hotel clerk watching us curiously and thought she must be her mother. So was the hotel run by a black family? Curiosity overcame my exhaustion and fear. It helped me to be able to focus on something else. I smiled over at the clerk, and she gave me a puzzled look before tentatively smiling back. Heaven knew who they thought I was, but I wanted to assure her that I was friendly. Being around black people who weren't slaves was foreign to me, but I was determined to open my mind and see them as the Occaneechi saw me. If I was going to live in the north, I needed to change my way of thinking. A small plate of johnnycakes with some milk and bread was brought to me a few minutes later. I looked at Priscilla in surprise.

"Is that supper?" I had been expecting a more substantial meal.

Priscilla shrugged and nodded apologetically.

"Yes, ma'am. We ran out of the mincemeat pies," she replied as though she expected me to snap at her.

I sighed deeply and smiled, reassuring her that the johnnycakes were fine. I didn't know what time it was, but I knew it was late if they were already out of supper. I was also too hungry to complain about any food and ate quickly. Once my stomach was appeased, even if not full, I stumbled up to my room. It was plain and bare of anything except a small bed with a woollen blanket, cotton pillow, and half-burnt candle on the dresser. I undressed, not bothering to light the candle. The moon shone bright enough through the tiny window to let in enough light for me to see by. I wrapped myself in the blanket, expecting sleep to consume me instantly, but my senses were too alert to the deep, drawling voices talking and singing outside. I worried about what the morning would bring and how I would find my way alone to New York in this inhospitable north.

Chapter Eleven

The next morning over a hearty breakfast of cornmeal mush with cream and maple syrup, I learned more about the hotel clerk and Priscilla. The clerk's name was Chaney, and I had been correct in my assumption that Priscilla was her daughter. They had travelled north from South Carolina a few years ago as freedom seekers when the war broke out. Priscilla had only been three years old, but Chaney lovingly stroked her daughter's hair as she said she had managed well. Her husband had gone before them, and through multiple avenues along the slave chain, word had reached them that he had managed to obtain freedom in Pennsylvania and to come north to him.

"Through God's blessings, we made it," Chaney finished, picking up my empty plate and wiping a firm hand down her apron front. "It's a hard life still, but we're free."

She held her head high and cocked it at me as if daring me to disagree. I had told her what little I could about myself, hesitant to admit that I came from a slave-holding family in Georgia. Chaney wasn't obtuse, and when I mentioned to her that I was from Atlanta, her wide-set nostrils flared, but she stayed quiet. My journey took her aback, especially when I mentioned staying with the Occaneechi, so she knew I wasn't pro-slavery, even though I wasn't an active abolitionist either. I didn't think Chaney knew what to make of me, but she was willing to be polite, which was all I asked for.

"You're doing a fine job here," I said kindly. "It must not be easy running a hotel."

"That it's not." Chaney shook her head ruefully but shrugged and flashed me a quick smile. "But it's what we have, and we'll make it the best we can."

I admired her spirit and optimism. My future in New York was uncertain, and I knew I could very well end up destitute, surviving on whatever means necessary. Although I hoped for better, hope didn't equal certainty. Whatever happened, I knew I wanted to have that same positive outlook on my life. Without it, I was sure she and Priscilla wouldn't have survived their own journey.

"You're going to New York?" Priscilla suddenly asked. Chaney had disappeared with my empty plate, but Priscilla stayed, too curious about me to leave.

"Yes, I am," I said happily, hoping my light tone would make the little girl more comfortable around me. "I've heard it's quite large."

Priscilla nodded fervently, her eyes round and her mouth hanging open slightly at the idea of such a big city.

"There are people here travelling there as well," she mentioned. "Maybe you can go with them."

I smiled at her innocence, thinking how easy life must seem to a child. Find a friend to travel with; it'll be no bother at all. I thanked her and told her I'd look into it. Satisfied with that response, she trotted away to the kitchen to help Chaney prepare dinner. I stood for a moment, trying to plan my next action before getting my rucksack. According to Chaney, New York City was a day's travel. My heart quickened with nervous excitement at the thought that my journey would soon be over. I could soon find High Bridge, the bridge the Spirits had shown me, and start a new life. As I headed for the stairs to collect my rucksack, Chaney suddenly appeared, standing beside a tall black man. His face was smooth from wrinkles, but the faded crow's feet around his eyes and deep crease between his brows made me think he might be in his early thirties. He was dressed in baggy trousers that were held up with suspenders and a loose-fitting cotton shirt adorned with a plain tie.

"Ora, this here is Hiram Baker," she said. "He's with a group travelling to New York today. I mentioned you, and he agreed you might be safer accompanying them than going alone."

For a brief second, I wondered if Priscilla had said anything to Chaney, but I didn't have time to ask. I smiled gratefully and nodded.

"Thank you for the kind offer; I would love to." I eyed Hiram with interest. He was unabashedly staring at me, obviously calculating what kind of person I was. "Please wait a moment while I gather my things."

I ascended the stairs, conscious of Hiram's eyes on my back. He unnerved me a little, but I didn't feel anything sinister from him, just pure curiosity.

Is he safe, Spirits? I asked, hoping they'd respond.

There was no reply, and I was apprehensive as I went back down the stairs. Perhaps this wasn't what the Spirits wanted me to do, but I couldn't wait for their response forever. I had to decide now. Hiram had joined his group already, so Chaney told me where they were, wishing me luck. I wished her the same and went to the group heading to New York. I did wonder why some of these men weren't fighting in the war. I knew many freed blacks had become Union soldiers. The group of around thirty people were gathered outside the hotel, and I was the last to join them. They were a hodgepodge made up of men, women, and children of all ages.

"Chaney said your name is Ora," Hiram said. He was a man with presence, with a long, wide nose and sharp-boned features. I could tell that he was the leader of this motley group, and everything was reported to him.

"Yes, Ora Harding," I replied. "Thank you for inviting me to join you."

He nodded thoughtfully and then gestured toward a few women and children gathered together.

"You're welcome. Chaney said as how you were alone. Y'can join my wife, Eliza, and our children."

Then he abruptly left to tend to other matters with the men. I hesitantly walked up to his wife and three children. The children were from five to ten years old and watched me with open suspicion, especially the oldest boy. He was the child version of his father and acted the part, leading his younger siblings. I smiled in amusement and then introduced myself to Eliza.

"Hello, I'm Ora," I said, "Hiram told me I could travel with you."

Eliza's dark brown eyes widened, and she looked behind me, craning her neck to see if her husband was in sight. From her surprised and dismayed expression, I understood why Hiram had chosen to go see the men. Not finding him, she looked at me with resignation and cocked an eyebrow.

"He did, did he?" she asked dryly. "Well, he's the boss; we listen to him. I'm Eliza, and these are our children, Solomon, Ned, and little Fanny."

She pointed to each child in turn, starting with the oldest boy. Solomon gave me a polite nod but didn't return my smile. The two younger children readily smiled, and the youngest, Fanny, came over to me. Her young face stirred the wound in my heart left by Leila, and my smile faded a bit as the pain tightened my throat.

"You're funny looking," she said brashly, earning her a cuff on the ear from her mother.

"Hush now," Eliza snapped in embarrassment. "We don't talk like that, y'hear?"

I chuckled and assured Eliza that no offence was taken.

"I am funny looking," I told Fanny, and Eliza narrowed her eyes at me. "I'm sure you've never seen moccasins before."

The children shook their heads, eyeing my footwear with curiosity. I welcomed them to take a closer look and feel them if they wanted. If I was going to travel with this family, then we needed to be comfortable with each other. Although I didn't hold any animosity towards these freed slaves, I wasn't used to living amongst freed black people. I had only ever talked to them as servants, although meeting Abner had eased some of my discomfort with speaking to them as equals. Fortunately, the children were a nice ice breaker for both Eliza and me.

"Your accent is from the south," I said to her, trying to come up with conversation while the children admired the moccasins. "Where did you travel from?"

Eliza hesitated for a moment. I could tell she didn't quite trust me, and I could scarcely blame her. An instinctive impatience at not getting an immediate response rose within me, but I forced it down.

"Florida," she finally said, her tone short. "This whole group is from the Carolinas, Georgia, or Florida. We're freed slaves from the Emancipation, and all made our way north. And you?"

Her tone was demanding, and the back of my neck prickled with irritation. I wasn't used to being spoken to like that. However, I also knew I needed to respect her and stop seeing her as a servant. We were equals now, and by all rights, she even owned more than I did.

"I'm from Atlanta," I replied. "My parents were killed escaping the city's surrender. I'm on my way to New York to find work."

My tone told her I wouldn't say more on the matter, and she frowned thoughtfully.

"Suppose you're not like most white women," she mused, taking in my attire. "Are you an abolitionist?"

I hadn't been prepared for this question, and my mouth dropped open.

"Not actively, but I won't own slaves again," I said delicately. "My life is in the north now."

She nodded slowly, considering this before finally looking back at me warmly.

"Then you're welcome to join my family," she offered, making me wonder if Hiram was really the one in charge or not. "We'll be leaving soon."

She was right. I could sense the sudden bustle of people gathering belongings, hitching wagons, and starting to move. Our day's journey was beginning, and I felt it was going to be a most interesting one. As I walked along with Eliza and the children, I wondered what possible conversation we could have. I had never spoken with a black person longer than necessary, even Phibe, so I wasn't sure what to say. For the first few hours, we were quiet, Eliza apparently having the same trouble I was. Though I was sure we were both curious about each other, neither wanted to be the first to pry. By this time, the children had grown tired, and Eliza had hoisted them into the back of a wagon.

There were only three wagons in the group, one filled with food supplies, one owned by a family, and the other with camping supplies since we would have to make camp right before reaching New York. I listened to the people chatting around us and noticed that they sounded very similar to the slaves we had owned. I had never been able to decipher exactly what it was our slaves were saying and had simply attributed it to not really listening. But now, even with my ears focused sharply on every word, I still couldn't quite make out what they were saying. In fact, it almost sounded like a different language entirely. This was confusing, especially since Eliza spoke to me quite clearly. I decided to break the silence and figured this was a good place to start a conversation.

"Are they speaking a different language?" I asked her, gesturing towards the people walking along with us.

Eliza turned to me in surprise, then chuckled, nodding.

"Yaas, madam," she said, her words drawled slow and long. "Sezzee say Gullah."

She laughed at my blank expression, her white teeth shining against her ebony skin. I smiled back timidly, hoping I hadn't looked offensive, but her response bewildered me.

"They're speaking Gullah," she clarified, a chuckle still deep in her throat. "This whole group is descended from the Gullah Geechee people brought over from Central and West Africa. When the different tribes were thrown together and then taught English, a new creole language was created so we could understand one another."

"But you don't speak it all the time?" I questioned. She obviously knew how to speak it, so I found it interesting that she wasn't using it like everyone else.

"Hiram and I are different," she said, sounding almost like she was confessing. "We didn't work in the fields. He was our master's personal servant, always running errands for him and such. I was the main housemaid, rearing the children and cooking. We needed to speak properly in the house and with the master, so we never used it as much as the others."

Her English was uneducated, but it was clear. She had been someone's Phibe, I realised. And, of course, it had never occurred to me that Phibe would speak any differently to us as she would to others. If Eliza was right, and the Gullah Geechee people had been in Georgia, as many of this group were my state's slaves, then Phibe had probably spoken Gullah as well. That explained why I could never quite understand them.

"I see," I said. "You had a culture."

Eliza looked at me quizzically, but I was having an epiphany. I had never seen our slaves as people of their own right. They were their own people from African tribal cultures that we had ignored. I thought of the Occaneechi and felt a deep sense of shame. Their culture was also being eroded slowly, not brutally crucified like the slaves' culture had been, but chipped away into nonexistence. Tears filled my eyes.

"I'm so sorry, Eliza," I whispered, my throat tightening with shame. "I truly had no idea."

Eliza smiled and placed a soft hand on my shoulder.

"Why would you?" she asked, shrugging. "Slave culture ain't no interest to a white woman. We did our work; you did yours. Now we're here."

I took her point. We had both done what the southern culture had demanded of us, but it didn't matter now. She was free, and I was learning. I smiled at her, grateful for her kindness, but I still felt a deep guilt at not understanding before. Suddenly, a man's strong voice burst through the chatter, singing loudly.

Kumbaya, my Lord, Kumbaya!
Kumbaya, my lord, Kumbaya!
Kumbaya, my lord, Kumbaya!
O Lord, Kumbaya.

The melody was lovely, slow and uplifting. I was reminded of church services again and felt a pang in my heart. Eliza joined in with the rest of the group. Most were off-key, but I could understand the tune well enough.

Someone's crying, Lord, Kumbaya!
Someone's crying, Lord, Kumbaya!
Someone's crying, Lord, Kumbaya!
O Lord, Kumbaya

110

Someone's singing, Lord, Kumbaya!
Someone's singing, Lord, Kumbaya!
Someone's singing, Lord, Kumbaya!
O Lord, Kumbaya

Someone's praying, Lord, Kumbaya!
Someone's praying, Lord, Kumbaya!
Someone's praying, Lord, Kumbaya!
O Lord, Kumbaya.

I listened quietly, enjoying the song and wondering what it meant. I could feel the music connect everyone as if it was part of their conversation. It lifted spirits, provided entertainment, and was a way for this large group to stay together. Several people clapped between choruses, dancing a few steps in the spirit of the music, reminding me of the celebration dance with the Occaneechi. I realised how little difference there was between the two groups. Both were tribal and had distinct cultures, only one had been annihilated before the other. As I listened to everyone, I wondered just how much of their culture had really died. Despite being owned and mistreated, this Gullah culture was still intact, kept alive by a stubborn pride that I myself had felt for my own southern culture. Was there truly any difference at all between me, the Occaneechi, or the freed slaves?

We're all the same, I thought, understanding clearly. *That's what Lincoln is fighting for. To free these people.*

I heard bell chimes and smiled. The Spirits were pleased that I'd finally understood. I wondered if this was why they wanted me to head north. Not because it was the safest place to be during the war, but because I was supposed to grow as a person and become kinder-hearted towards all people, not only those I was used to.

"Always feel better with music," Eliza said jovially, her face beaming as she looked at me. The singing had stopped, and everyone was once again enjoying happy conversations as we made our way up the road.

"That was a lovely song," I said. "What does it mean?"

"Kumbaya means 'come by here' in Gullah," Eliza explained. "We're asking the good Lord to come by us."

I remembered our slaves singing as they worked, but again, I had never paid much attention. Partly because I couldn't understand them, but also because I didn't care. I'd heard it as mindless singing in the background of my busy life.

"It's a beautiful song," I repeated, not knowing what else to say through my guilt. I was feeling humbled, and this must have shown on my face. Eliza placed a chubby arm around my shoulders and squeezed.

"Don't you be worryin' honey," she said firmly. "Listen, we're happy people now. We're all goin' to New York for one reason or another. Some to join family, others to sign up with the Union, and others because they couldn't find work in Philadelphia. We're all movin' on with our lives. You are too."

I gave her a warm smile, thanked her, and we changed the subject to talk about my travels. I didn't mind sharing more with her now that she understood I wasn't a true Confederate. She gasped in horror about Leila and was interested to hear my story about Abner in Lynchburg. The afternoon rolled by quickly with us talking, breaking only to have a brief dinner of beans and cornmeal cakes before moving on. By dusk, Eliza's talking slowed, and we were enjoying a companionable silence, broken only by the needs of children and others coming by to drop in a word. I was pleased that Solomon had slowly warmed up to me, giving me a shy smile every once in a while. When darkness fell, my throat was dry from thirst and my legs were aching. I was just starting to wonder when we would make camp when I saw one of the men stop Hiram ahead of us.

"Figger we c'have a saa'bis come middlenight," the man said quickly, and Hiram nodded in agreement.

Before I could ask Eliza what he had said, Hiram walked up to us. He had been busy checking up on everyone throughout the day, minding that the wagons were fine and keeping an overall eye on everything.

"Toby thinks we should have service," he explained, and Eliza nodded quickly. "It's nearly midnight now, so we should make camp."

This order spread like lightning, and everyone was relieved to stop. We stepped off the road and found a wide clearing surrounded by thick forest. The camp consisted of several tents for families and a few campfires. Some of the single men simply rolled out bedrolls under the stars, but I was relieved to be offered a tent with Eliza and the children, with Hiram graciously offering to sleep outside. I thought it incredibly gentlemanly of him and told him so. He shrugged sheepishly. We filled our plates at the food wagon. Supper wasn't anything more than dried pork, hardtack pudding, and milk toast.

"Suppose I'd better get used to a soldier's rations," Hiram said as he filled his tin plate. "This kind of food is easiest to travel with."

The food surprised me a bit, but his explanation made sense.

"Are you joining up then?" I asked him as we returned to his family, who were sitting near a campfire. The children were half-asleep but managing to eat, wrapped in blankets. He sat next to Eliza and sighed before answering.

"Yes," he said, his voice deep with determination. "Me and some others are goin' to try to join the 26th New York Infantry regiment for coloured folk."

He gave a half-crooked smile at Eliza, who looked at him proudly and hugged his arm.

"We'll be in New York tomorrow morning at some point," he continued. "Where are you heading to, Ora?"

I sighed deeply, the imminent arrival in New York weighing heavily on me.

"High Bridge," I replied, knowing this sounded strange. "It's the only place I know of."

They looked at me in bewilderment but smiled politely. A laugh bubbled in my throat at their blank expressions.

"Well, not the bridge itself," I clarified, "but a place near it. I'm hoping to find work."

This seemed to make more sense to them.

"Shouldn't be hard," Eliza said, "I've heard there's loads of work there. D'you have a place to stay?"

I shook my head, which made her immediately frown. She turned to Hiram.

"We can't be lettin' her go wanderin' 'round the city without help," she told him, then turned back to

me. "We'll help you find a place before leavin'
you."

Warm gratitude filled me, and I thanked her
profusely. I was too nervous about the next day to
protest, especially after my experience with
northerners so far. There wasn't a guarantee that I
wouldn't be denied accommodation due to my
accent again. It made me appreciate the freed slave's
position even more. Both were discriminated
against.

The service Toby had requested was a rough
version of the services we would have back home,
punctuated with random shouts and stamps from
some of the men and women, and an almighty cry of
't'engk'gawd!' at the end. It held a special poignant
meaning that I had always missed in church. There I
had been safe with my family, surrounded by the
familiar sounds and comforts of home. But here in
the wilderness, accompanied by people I was only
just getting accustomed to, praying to God held
more importance, and my prayers became much
more fervent. Hiram acted as preacher and led the
prayers, his deep voice echoing through the dark
forest. I wasn't sure if it was due to being under the
stars or feeling the close camaraderie of everyone
around the crackling fire, but it was easier to feel
closer to God when praying this way. As we settled
in for a short night's sleep, my mind wandered
fitfully from home, to the Occaneechi, then to the
Gullah Geechee. By the time my dreams came to
me, I was hosting a dinner party in my old family
home, dressed in my mother's finest antebellum
dress. Eliza was singing in Gullah, and Briton and
Sarah were dancing in full Occaneechi attire around

the dining table. I smiled in my sleep, happy that we were all together.

Chapter Twelve

Dark clouds rolled steadily in as we made our final push into New York City. We left at daybreak after a hurried breakfast of cornmeal cakes. Many of the men had been looking at the sky, shaking their heads and worrying about the weather. A damp mist had settled in the forest during the night, but it had been blown away by a sharp wind that cut straight through our clothes. I couldn't tell exactly what month we were in now, but the weather made it clear winter was coming fast. One of the men had come up to Hiram by the end of breakfast, shaking his head and rolling his lips with concern.

"Uh don' luk t'at win', Ham," he grumbled, his thick brows furrowed. "Uh t'ink t'er's t'unduh in t'is col'."

I had looked to Eliza for interpretation. Apparently, the man was worried about the wind and thought there might be a storm coming. To my relief, we made it to New York before the storm, though I could feel its ominous presence coming in fast behind us. The wind was starting to whistle, and a light rain was just beginning to drop when the group stepped into the city.

I wasn't sure what I had expected New York to be, but the heavens didn't open with angels singing as I looked upon the rows of grey cobblestone streets lined with solid, formidable buildings. It was a vast jungle of intertwining streets and alleyways cornered by a mixture of small tenant homes and huge brick warehouses. Chaotic noise and crowds of people pushing and running everywhere overwhelmed me. For a brief moment, I wondered if I would be able to follow through with what the Spirits wanted me to do.

Everyone said a quick goodbye and went their own way. Hiram and Eliza stayed true to their word and stayed with me as we searched for High Bridge. Fortunately, it was a well-known spot, but getting directions wasn't so easy. It took several tries since many had given us a raised brow in criticism and walked on. I knew we seemed an unlikely group. A freed black family and a white southern woman dressed in rabbit fur and moccasins didn't exactly inspire people to talk to us. Only the newspaper boys were willing to offer directions. This cold greeting didn't provide me with any comfort that this would be my new home.

"Why High Bridge again?" Eliza asked, and I could tell from her weary tone that she was starting to question her Christian hospitality of escorting me here. The weather worried her too, and they still needed to get to their own destination.

"It was the only place I knew," I replied apologetically. "I can follow the directions on my own now if you'd like to meet up with the regiment."

I could see this suggestion tempted Eliza greatly. She kept looking at her children, huddled close together from the cold. I didn't want to keep them out here longer than necessary, and I didn't know how far the regiment was from here.

"I don't like leavin' you, but the children are gettin' cold," Hiram said gravely. I could tell he was torn on what to do, but I placed a reassuring hand on his arm and looked at him earnestly.

"I'll be fine," I said firmly. "Thank you so much for all your generosity. I'll find it from here, and you can get the children out of the weather."

He smiled gratefully, but had one piece of advice before he left.

"Find a boarding house," he said. "They're more likely to take in outcasts."

They left, waving until they turned the next corner. A sinking qualm settled in my stomach as I realised that I was alone once more. I was also getting tired of feeling like an outcast. As I followed the directions to continue down the main road, which was incredibly crowded and noisy, I took stock of my personal state. My clothes were sticky with sweat and dirt. I hadn't changed into my spares for at least a week, trying to salvage the clothes as long as I could. Dark tendrils of hair had escaped from their pins, and I could feel my hair starting to fall down my neck. I knew I looked like a ragamuffin and decided to tidy myself as best I could before trying to find a boarding house. No reason to give them more excuses to turn me away. Southerner or not, I at least had to look halfway respectable. I found a shop sitting next to an alleyway and surreptitiously used the window to tuck my hair into place. My face looked pale and gaunt from exhaustion and weeks of travelling. I stared for a moment at my reflection, and then stepped back out onto the crowded streets.

High Bridge soon came into view, and I nearly cried at the sight of it. Weeks of having a vague idea of what it was didn't prepare me for it in real life. It was a tall bridge, worthy of its name, with high stone arches supporting it like a Roman aqueduct, just like the Spirits had shown me. Construction works were being carried out on it, obviously building a walkway for pedestrians. They were in the final stages, and I was happy that I would get a chance to enjoy the fruit of the worker's labour. Unfortunately, the bridge didn't provide shelter from the rain and sleet that was now starting to fall in earnest. The storm was no longer a threat but a promise.

High Bridge was a wonderful landmark but useless for accommodation. It lay a little outside the main city, so I had to walk back to the busy streets, with the sleet pattering my frozen face.

"I just had to see the bridge," I scolded myself, my muttered words being whipped away by the wind. "I couldn't have just seen it as a landmark."

I should have listened to Hiram's advice and found a boarding house immediately. People quickly tried to find shelter, escaping into any building they could. I decided to fight the cold and continue my search, not wanting to delay any longer. My rabbit shawl warmed my shoulders, but nothing else. I finally came to a brownstone square building on a corner with a large Union flag waving on the roof. A small sign saying 'Boarding House' was hung to the side of the double front door.

I stood for a moment, not caring about the cold or sleet as I stared with mixed emotions at the Union flag. Its red and white stripes with a blue circle of stars caused a wave of resentment in me that I knew I needed to stifle before walking into the building. I understood now why Lincoln was waging his war against the Confederates, and I could possibly even sympathize with him, but the Union had taken my family, and I wasn't sure how much understanding could outweigh that entirely.

Enter now, the Spirits suddenly encouraged, and I took a deep breath and stepped inside.

A wave of warmth immediately cascaded over me, and I didn't care about the Union flag anymore. I was consumed with a ravenous desire for food, a bath, and clean clothes. I felt absolutely rank and wouldn't have blamed the boarding house owner for kicking me out for my poor hygiene alone. Several people wandered through the front rooms, mainly single men and women. I stood uncertainly, not sure where to go. Unlike a hotel, there wasn't a front desk to go to. I stood in a spacious front hall that opened onto a large sitting room furnished with emerald-green sofas and dark wood tables. The walls were dark mahogany and lined with cream wainscoting. A large fireplace held a roaring fire that illuminated the patterned carpet in front of it. After a few moments, an older woman approached me, her stern face set in a mask of sharp accusation.

"May I help you?" she snapped, her tone barely polite. "Dinner has to be served soon, so I don't have much time."

I hesitated briefly, wishing I didn't sound southern, but answered as clearly as I could.

"I need a room," I said quickly, hoping to mask my accent by talking fast.

The woman paused, taking me in with a cursory look.

"Are you alone?" she asked, raising an eyebrow critically. I couldn't decide if she expected me to be young enough to need parents.

"I am," I said shortly. "I'm here to find work and need a place to stay."

A man's boisterous laugh sounded loudly from the adjoining room, reminding the woman of her dinner duties. She flicked a glance towards the sound and then looked back at me, her lips pursed.

"Alright," she said firmly. "I'll take you in, though I know you're a southerner. My name is Ms Hall. You can pay five dollars and fifty cents weekly. That includes three meals a day plus laundry service. I'll show you to a room. Is this all you have?"

She pointed at my rucksack, and I nodded. She gave a throaty 'hmph' under her breath, turned quickly, and marched up the red-carpeted stairs, speaking in a rushed tone.

"The room is expected to be kept tidy and intact," Ms Hall instructed firmly. "Any damage you have to pay for. Otherwise, breakfast is at seven, dinner at one, and supper at five. If you miss it, then you're on your own. Any questions?"

Aside from how on earth I was supposed to pay that much per week, everything seemed clear. I shook my head, and Ms Hall continued.

"We're a nice establishment here, so no nightly means of earning an income," she said, and I flushed with her meaning. "What's your name?"

"Ora Harding," I murmured, completely intimidated by this formidable, strict woman.

"Well, Miss Harding, I hope you enjoy your stay," she said shortly and walked from the room.

Once the door was shut behind her, I let out the breath that had been trapped in my chest.

So much for warm hospitality, I thought, missing the kind, cordial nature of the south. The north seemed so much colder, and not just from the weather. No one down south would have greeted

122

someone with such a stern and unfriendly demeanour, especially a paying guest!

Taking off my rucksack, I looked around the room that was now my home for the indeterminable future. It was spacious enough, with a good-sized double bed and comfortable bedclothes. A solid wood chest of drawers sat against the far wall with a tall matching wardrobe beside it. On the wall next to the door to my left was a vanity table, complete with a large mirror. I had to admit that it was a decent room for five dollars and fifty cents per week, even though the thought of paying that price was overwhelming. I would need to find work immediately.

My heart sank as I sat down on the bed to undress. There was a ewer and basin on the chest of drawers for bathing, along with a linen towel and bar of soap. As I undressed, I noticed the disgraceful state of my clothes. My eyes filled with tears, and I nearly started sobbing. How was I supposed to find work when I didn't even have proper clothing? The moccasins had been a lifesaver while travelling, but I would need a good pair of shoes to find work. I emptied my rucksack, unpacking what little I had. My spare clothes were still in decent wear, so I decided to wear them down to dinner. The others were so poorly off that I hoped they were even salvageable. I covered the bed with the woollen blanket Abner had given me, glad to have the extra warmth for winter. Once I bathed as best I could, I felt a bit better. I combed my hair, twisted it into a neat bun, dressed in my fresh change of clothes, and ruefully put the moccasins back on. Shoes were going to have to be my first purchase. With this thought, I sat down to count the money I had left. I knew it couldn't be much and was right. I only had two dollars left to my name. Before my panicked tears could escape, I stood up and went down to dinner.

The dining room was filled with people, but thankfully no one took notice of me as I sat down at the long table. They were too busy talking with one another or eating with their own thoughts. Another stranger coming into the room was expected. This comforted me, since the last thing I wanted was to be the centre of attention. Everyone was dressed in nice attire, many of the men in business suits and a woman in a lovely daytime dress. Now that I was in a respectable house, I felt like a street urchin and unfit for polite company because of my wrinkled clothing and strange footwear. Ms Hall brought me a plate, and the scent of food made me forget anything else. It was a mincemeat pie with a side of boiled potatoes. She gave me a quick smile before marching off again, and I hoped that perhaps her strictness had simply been because she was in a hurry. I quickly began eating and looked up to find a man sitting across from me, watching me with an amused expression.

"If you're lucky, there will be a slice of rhubarb pie to follow," he said kindly. His steel-blue eyes were warm and friendly, and his tone soft.

"Thank you, that would be wonderful," I said, taking another bite.

He didn't say anything else, and I ate the rest of my dinner in silence, watching the people sitting with me. I was only one of two women; the rest were men ranging from early twenties to mid-fifties. The other woman was young but possibly a few years older than me. The rumble of conversation didn't interest me as it was mainly political. The man sitting across from me wasn't part of it. He was enjoying contented silence, happy to smoke his pipe and listen. When Ms Hall saw I was finished, she brought out the slice of pie he had mentioned. He smiled at me when she put it down.

"Ms Hall makes the best rhubarb pie," he told me before giving Ms Hall a charming wink.

"Oh, stop now," she snapped, but her lips turned up in an amused grin. "If you're done with your dinner, Mr Crowly, I suggest you move on to let another have your seat."

He gave a quick nod, taking her advice, and stood. He turned to me and bowed shortly.

"Pardon me, miss," he said formally, and my stomach somersaulted. I hadn't been addressed formally in what seemed ages. I almost forgot my manners entirely, but I smiled and nodded before he walked away.

The slice of pie was gone in four bites since I was so hungry. I was walking back to my room when I noticed Mr Crowly lounging in one of the wing-tipped chairs in the sitting room, smoking his pipe with his legs crossed comfortably. I had contemplated sitting by the fire, but he looked so peaceful I didn't want to disturb him. Before I could walk past the room to the stairs, he called out to me.

"You're welcome to join me if you wish," he offered in a light tone. "The fire is much warmer than the rooms upstairs."

I smiled graciously, feeling as if he had read my mind. I felt self-conscious in my moccasins and wished I looked more formal. Mr Crowly seemed to be a gentleman, dressed smartly in a suit with a neatly trimmed beard. It was difficult to judge, but I thought him to be in his mid-twenties. He flashed me a warm smile as I sat on the sofa across from his chair, sitting as straight and properly as I could.

"I appreciate the offer," I said smoothly, determined to sharpen my etiquette skills again. "I didn't wish to disturb you."

"Not at all; I like the company," he said, his smile making my stomach squirm again. "May I ask your name?"

I told him, and he sat back, nodding with polite interest. A plume of smoke rose from his lips as he responded.

"A lovely name," he said. "I'm Harold Crowly, Miss Harding. You're obviously from the south."

An implied question lifted his tone, and I could tell he was burning with curiosity but didn't want to be too forward. I hesitated, then decided it was best to be upfront. After all, I could hardly disguise my accent.

"Yes, though I'm hoping to find work here soon," I said, not wanting to go into detail. "Do you happen to know of any factories that will take female workers?"

Mr Crowly's eyes widened, and I had surprised him enough for his pipe to fall into his fingers. He regarded me with even further interest, taking in my attire and manners, and then frowned.

"You act like a lady," he said, thoughtfully tapping his pipe against his teeth. "I can't imagine you in factory work."

"Be that as it may," I said firmly, "I'm not in a position at the moment to rely on a lady's charms to

126

pay my way. I need to find work quickly so I can pay Ms Hall."

I stared at him, my lips pursed with annoyance. I didn't know what he was implying by thinking I couldn't work in a factory, but I didn't like to be dissuaded from my plans. Mr Crowly's lips quivered with an amused chuckle, and he smiled, showing a neat line of white teeth.

"Understandable," he said. "There are many seamstress factories around here. Can you sew?"

His tone was mocking, and his eyes were sparkling with laughter. I was suddenly becoming tired of him.

"I can learn to work any machine," I snapped, my manners starting to crumble. "I know how the factories work. My mother used to work in them when she was young. I can be taught to do anything."

Mr Crowly's smile faded, and his eyes softened.

"I apologise, Miss Harding; I've offended you," he said warmly. "I wish you the best of luck in finding work. I don't know of any particular factory, but there are many to try around here. I won't trouble you longer."

He stood, gave a short bow, and left the room before I could respond. I felt bewildered and slightly guilty for my angry response. I sat for a moment, struggling to control my emotions that seemed scattered everywhere. I hadn't spoken with a young, attractive man since my last ball in Atlanta, and I didn't even want to think how many months it had been since then. Suddenly, I knew I couldn't let him leave without an apology of my own. I rushed after him, catching him at the foot of the stairs. He turned around when I said his name, his face pleasantly surprised.

"I owe you an apology," I said quickly, my cheeks burning with embarrassment. "I had no reason to snap at you like that. I've been travelling for twenty-four days, and I'm frightened about finding work and paying Ms Hall. I haven't slept well in days, and New York is just overwhelming, all of the north is, and I think when you said I couldn't find work, I just snapped."

I realised I was starting to blabber with overwrought emotion, but once I began to explain, the words seemed to pour out of me. I shut my mouth firmly. Mr Crowly's blue eyes were wide with amazement. He took the pipe slowly out of his mouth and looked at me with a gentle expression. It was affectionate and understanding. It also made my knees like water.

"I appreciate your concern for my feelings, Miss Harding," he said softly, the whisper of a chuckle underlying his tone. "It sounds as if you've had quite a long journey. I would love to hear about it if you ever feel the need."

My cheeks flushed with pleasure, and I nodded, unable to turn my eyes from him.

"That would be lovely," I said, surprised to find that I actually looked forward to telling him. He was easy to talk to and a natural listener.

He took his leave, and I was sorry to see him go. I could only hope that he would be around the boarding house long enough to become a friend. As I watched him ascend the stairs, I heard bells chime in my ear and smiled. My Spirits liked him too.

Chapter Thirteen

S now flurries fell lightly on the glass-pane
window of my room, outlining the edges,
making it look like a large, delicate snowflake.
I quickly dressed for the day, knowing I needed to
hurry to make breakfast on time. A month had
passed since I had arrived at the boarding house, and
the Christmas season had arrived. I hated the
reminders of the festive holiday, thinking of my
family and home before the war broke out. I would
miss seeing Leila's face on Christmas morning,
Mama singing carols at the piano, and Papa carrying
the large baked ham while Phibe followed with
oysters, potatoes, and cabbage. Of course, Christmas
had been less merry the past few years due to
blockades, but when I thought of Christmas, I
couldn't help but remember the good memories. My
chest tightened as I thought about it, and I had to sit
on the bed to calm my thoughts.

Stop remembering, I told myself firmly. *It doesn't
do any good.*

With this strict order, I collected myself,
continuing to dress. I tightened my corset over my
chemise, put on my blue day dress, and pulled on
my high-topped boots, lacing the sides. I took the
time to admire my new clothes in the mirror, happily
feeling like a proper woman again. Mr Crowly had
surprised me with them a couple of days after I
arrived. He had insisted that if I were to seriously
pursue employment, I needed to be dressed the part.
I had been speechless with gratitude, but he had

shaken his head when I tried to say anything. Even a few weeks later, I wondered how I would pay him back. I still kept my moccasins and rucksack together, knowing that the memories they held would forever be special to me.

After a week of searching for factory work, I had given up. None of the factories had been generous enough to offer employment to a southerner. I had paid Ms Hall my two dollars, promising fervently to pay the rest when I found employment. It had taken every ounce of courage I had, and her flared nostrils and tight lips had sent a cold fear over me. But she had accepted it, stating she didn't wish a young lady to become homeless. However, I knew she had watched me carefully that first week, ensuring I was looking for work as promised. Once I had given up on the factories, I felt dejected and close to giving up. A person could only be turned down so many times before losing heart entirely.

Visit the army, the Spirits had suddenly said one day.

Hearing them had awakened my determination again, and I went to the Union army, asking to be a laundress. They paid little but would take anyone, and ironically seemed grateful for the help, even from a southerner. Every penny I made went to Ms Hall, but since I had few other prospects, I knew I was at least lucky enough to be able to pay for room and board.

I walked down the stairs quickly, brushing a hand over my hair to ensure everything was in place. It felt wonderful to look respectable again, and the few weeks of working as a laundress had strengthened my self-confidence. I hadn't the slightest clue what else I was going to do with my life, but for the moment, I was keeping myself afloat.

"Good morning, Miss Harding," Mr Crowly said warmly, greeting me at the dining table as he always did. "I trust you slept well?"

"As always, Mr Crowly," I replied happily. It gave me a giddy pleasure to see him every morning, though knowing this concerned me.

He and I had become fast friends as I had hoped, often spending the evenings together in the sitting room. I learned that he was actually from New Hampshire and was here to visit an old business acquaintance who was in need of a solicitor. I found him to be well-educated, intelligent, and kind, with a quick wit and patience that I respected. Our conversations flowed naturally, and even after telling him of my journey from Atlanta, he had listened with genuine interest, not simply being polite. My story had fascinated him, and ever since, he had treated me with even more attention.

"Your bravery is remarkable," he had said, and I have treasured those words ever since. They meant a lot to me, knowing they weren't spoken lightly coming from him.

I found Mr Crowly to be genuine and honest, and that his silence simply meant that nothing needed to be said. He was a refreshing change from the loud-spoken, hot-headed young men I had known before, always boasting about their achievements or getting temperamental over politics. Even when men at the dining table became overly boisterous, Mr Crowly would sit silently, patiently waiting for a calm moment before voicing his opinion, if necessary. I admired his calm patience.

"Are you working today?" he asked as we sat down for breakfast.

I nodded, and my heart started hammering nervously. Was today the day he would break the news that he was leaving? I knew he would go back home eventually, and had actually been surprised that he had stayed as long as he had.

"Yes, though I'll be home by evening," I said, hoping that he would respond as he always did and would be in the sitting room waiting for me.

"I'm leaving tomorrow," he said sadly, his blue eyes staring at me intently.

For a brief second, my heart stopped entirely, and I felt tears rise. Mr Crowly was my only friend here. Without him, I would be completely alone once more.

"What time?" I asked, my voice hardly going over a whisper due to the lump in my throat.

"In the afternoon at two o'clock," he replied softly, and then to my shock, he boldly reached out and took me by the hand, squeezing it tightly.

I dropped my fork in surprise, but the intensity of his gaze and the warm strength of his grip prevented me from speaking.

"I was most fervently hoping," he began, his tone so nervous that he was nearly stammering, "that you would agree to accompany me back to New Hampshire."

This shocked me completely. My mind raced. Leave New York? This was where the Spirits had told me to go. Leave my work? I had finally found employment and was getting on my feet. But be alone? I glanced around the dining room and towards the front hall. This boarding house was hardly home, and I dreaded the thought of being alone in it without the comfort of him.

"Why?" I finally asked, landing on the only question I could form coherently.

Mr Crowly licked his lips, set down his pipe, and looked at me, his expression more serious than I had ever seen.

"I have enjoyed our friendship this past month implicitly," he explained firmly, though his tone was gentle. "You are a well-educated and well-bred lady with no business working as a laundress. Miss Harding, you're worth more than that. Especially for me."

I was burning with warmth from his complimentary words but frowned at the last in confusion.

"For you?" I asked, cocking my head slightly.

"Yes, for me," he said and sat up, releasing my hand. He looked nervous, and I suddenly suspected he had something important to say. "I have not been entirely honest with you regarding my situation. I am from New Hampshire, and I am visiting a business acquaintance. But there's more than that."

The creamed porridge I was eating curled in my stomach at this, and I turned cold. I prepared myself for some horrible truth he was about to confess. His face was white with nerves.

"I see," I said, hoping I sounded calmer than I felt. "Why wouldn't you be honest with me? Especially after I confided my entire story to you."

I could feel angry tears forming and tried to stop them, but his betrayal was painful. I had felt I knew him, that he was good and trustworthy, but he had been hiding a secret. I wanted to walk out of the room. He must have seen this, for he immediately

133

took my hand again, his face determined and his voice pleading.

"Listen, please," he said quickly. "It isn't what you must think. I didn't tell you because I didn't want to frighten you. I enjoyed your company too much to risk losing it. I'm a widower and have two young daughters, aged five and seven. Their mother died in childbirth, and I have been struggling to raise them on my own. My housekeeper, Polly, does what she can to help, but they need a well-educated woman to be their governess. I was hoping you would accept the position."

My head whirled. This was far too heavy of a conversation for the breakfast table. I needed air and fast. I abruptly left the table, but Mr Crowly followed me. The other boarders watched us with mild interest, but I didn't care. Thoughts raced as fast as my feet, and I found myself outside on the stoop, inhaling cold air in quick gasps as snow flurries settled on my shoulders.

"Why do you think that would frighten me?" I said angrily, whirling on Mr Crowly when he joined me. "Did you think I was too young to understand?"

He sighed heavily and shook his head.

"Not at all," he replied dryly. "On the contrary, you're mature for your years. It was because I wanted to know you better before admitting that I was a widower. I needed to be sure that you were as wonderful as I suspected, and I've found that you are, Miss Harding. You're exactly what I need for my girls."

I felt a warm flush rise from my chest to my cheeks at this but stubbornly refused to let go of my anger.

"I see," I said, my tone short but controlled. "I appreciate your offer, Mr Crowly, but I'll have to think about this carefully. I'll give you an answer by morning."

I turned to go back inside but was stopped by a firm, gentle grip on my upper arm.

"I treasure our friendship, Miss Harding," he said. "Please, I don't want to lose it."

My anger melted slightly at his warm eyes and determined tone. A part of me would have happily agreed to follow him anywhere, but the other part hesitated, not quite sure if that's what I was meant to do.

"I don't want to lose it either," I agreed softly, and his immediate smile nearly took my breath away. "But give me time to think about this. I've never been a governess."

I left then to finish my breakfast and head for work. There was a lot to think about.

My arms quivered with exhaustion from lifting soggy, heavy clothes and bed linens all day by the time I made my way back to the boarding house that evening. One nice part of being a laundress was that it didn't require much mental attention. My mind was free, and I'd thought of nothing else but Mr Crowly. I had tried asking the Spirits, but of course, they were silent. I noticed they only came to me on their terms, not mine, which was quite annoying.

As I walked through the busy streets, I still pondered my answer. Mr Crowly was a truly remarkable man and a close friend in such a short time. I had to admit that being a governess to two girls was certainly more promising than lifting heavy laundry all day. The skin on my hands was cracked and sore from being constantly wet, and I was tired of trudging the long distance to the army camp daily. So was my only hesitation due to the Spirits telling me to come here? I was starting to think that perhaps it was time to let go of the Spirits and make my own decisions. They weren't guiding me much anymore, and this seemed too large of a decision to wait on them for.

I even ask you, and you don't answer, I thought irritably, kicking a stone out of my way on the dirt road.

No, this was a decision I had to make alone. At last, I entered the boarding house, rubbing my arms from the cold and unbuttoning my coat, another gift from Mr Crowly. I rubbed the woollen fabric between my fingers thoughtfully. He would make a good employer, I had no doubt. He was patient, fair, and listened well. We were good friends and would most likely work well together. If I could forgive his secrecy, then I felt this prospect was entirely agreeable.

I went upstairs to freshen up before supper. I stared at myself in the vanity mirror and took a deep breath. Deep inside, I knew his secrecy hadn't been that terrible, and he had an understandable reason for wanting to know me better before offering me a governess position. I was practical enough to understand that. I couldn't use his secrecy as an excuse to cover my fear of leaving the stability of New York. If I was honest with myself, there wasn't much stability in being a laundress and living in a boarding house.

"I guess I'm going to New Hampshire," I told my reflection, and giggled at the idea of it.

Now that I had firmly decided, I felt a heavy weight lift and a bubble of happiness rise in its wake. I was going to be a governess. That was a proper job, and the idea of raising two little girls warmed my heart.

I rushed downstairs for supper, nearly colliding with a few boarders who snapped at me impatiently. I didn't care. All I wanted was to see Mr Crowly's young, kind face and give him the good news. He was already sitting at the dining table, smoking his pipe, his face tight with nerves. I walked up to him, and his eyes widened when he saw me.

"I wasn't sure I would see you this evening after what happened this morning," he admitted, a concerned wrinkle creasing his forehead.

"Mr Crowly," I began formally, a wide grin spreading across my face, "I would be honoured to accept your offer."

His worried features immediately lightened into an elated expression, his eyes shining with relief. I felt wonderful making him so happy.

"Thank you, Miss Harding," he said with breathless excitement. "I can scarcely believe it."

As I sat across from him, I heard bells chime in my ear, and the last part of me that was hesitant relaxed fully.

Finally, I thought, and raised my glass to Mr Crowly in a toast.

Chapter Fourteen

It was a three-day journey north to New Hampshire. Even though it was still winter, we travelled in Mr Crowly's carriage. I had asked about possibly taking a train, but Mr Crowly had given a bemused chuckle, stating that there weren't any railroads yet in New Hampshire. This astounded me and made me wonder what sort of wild frontier state I was heading for. Along with concerns about the cold weather, I also had reservations about travelling alone with a man for such a long time. By her appalled and austere expression, Ms Hall felt the same way when I told her my plans. However, she had begrudgingly agreed that Mr Crowly was a respectable man, and our fears were proven unnecessary on the trip. Mr Crowly remained a faithful gentleman, making sure I had a room of my own every time we stopped at an inn. To his amusement, I had brought my rucksack to carry my belongings, refusing to let him buy me proper luggage.

"This rucksack has worked well for me from North Carolina," I told him firmly. "My friends with the Occaneechi gave it to me as a gift, and I intend to honour them by using it."

With a smirk, he hadn't argued, but his eyes had softened, and he had squeezed my shoulder gently.

"You're right to use it," he agreed, and never brought it up again.

I had, however, allowed him to buy me a few outfits so I could be appropriately fitted out when meeting his household. I certainly didn't want to appear as some beggar woman he had picked up off the streets. Fortunately, the three days of travel passed uneventfully, and I found that spending the extra time with Mr Crowly was highly pleasant, and he made an enjoyable travelling companion. When we arrived at his home, I had briefly worried about what his housekeeper, Polly, might think of me being a southerner. I couldn't help but confide my concern to Mr Crowly, who paused thoughtfully.

"There is a difference between a Confederate and a southerner," he said carefully, and I could see he didn't want to offend me. "Would you say you're still a Confederate?"

"Not after all I've been through," I stated firmly, "but I'll always be a southerner."

"Then you have no cause to worry," he assured me.

I had misgivings about this logic, but Mr Crowly was proven right when I met Polly. She was an older woman in her fifties, robust, short, and her face as weathered as an old apple. She had beamed with unadulterated delight at meeting me, clapping her hands excitedly as we drove up to the house, which was a solid, two-storey wooden clapboard structure with a wraparound porch. It was nothing fancy, but it was large, and I knew Mr Crowly earned a decent living to afford the upkeep of such a home.

"Lord have mercy, you made it home!" she squealed with glee. "And who is this lovely young woman?"

"Our new governess," Mr Crowly replied proudly, introducing me. "This is Miss Ora Harding."

Introductions were made in a whirlwind of excited cries, hugs, and assurances to the two shy girls who appeared in the front doorway, their eyes wide with surprise and anxiety. They had pretty features that made me think their mother must have been quite beautiful. I immediately walked up to them, my heart squeezing painfully at the sight of the youngest one's face. She reminded me of Leila, only a year older with blonde curls and blue eyes instead of light brown. I almost couldn't breathe as I knelt down to talk to her.

"Hello, what's your name?" I said quietly, feeling the urge to twirl one of her ringlets around my finger.

"Caroline," she whispered, hugging a stuffed doll against her tightly.

"I'm Hannah," the older one volunteered, her shyness disappearing after her sister had spoken. Her hair was a light chestnut colour, and her eyes were hazel.

"It's lovely meeting you both," I smiled warmly. I couldn't wait to start working with them.

We entered the house then, and I was shown my room next to the nursery where the girls slept. Mr Crowly kept quite a comfortable home, and I was reminded of my old home in Atlanta, only on a simpler scale. By suppertime, the girls had relaxed enough to want to talk, which Mr Crowly happily allowed, sitting in quiet amusement as the girls pelted me with questions. They hadn't seen a young woman in a long time and were rapt with interest. My stories and southern accent delighted them, and they were willing to laugh as easily as their father. Polly joined in as she served the next course, which surprised me at first. I wasn't used to the help talking, but I found that I preferred it since Polly was an interesting woman in her own right.

Once supper was over, Mr Crowly brought me to his study to discuss the details of my employment. This hadn't taken long, and we soon lapsed into more casual conversation.

"How do you like it?" he asked curiously, his eyes hopeful.

"Your home is beautiful," I said warmly. "The girls are darlings, and I can't wait to work with them. Thank you for bringing me here."

His cheeks flushed, and he gently smiled.

"The girls are happy you're here too," he said. "Thank you for coming."

We laughed a bit, both feeling an unusual awkwardness between us, but not an uncomfortable one. I couldn't quite place what caused it, but I thought it might simply be from mutual happiness.

It was the middle of spring, and bursts of purple, white, and yellow flowers were just beginning to blossom, outlining the pockets of snow that were quickly melting. This was my favourite time of year, watching the world be reborn around me. Spring in the north was very different, filled with crocuses, tulips, and daffodils instead of the more tropical azaleas, hyacinths, and Spanish bluebells I was used to in the south. The temperature was also different, only warm enough to melt winter's frost instead of the balmy promise of summer's humidity. The girls and I had become quite close, with Caroline particularly endeared to me. She tended to follow me around, always wanting to ask a question or play, and I was happy to indulge her. Having her in my life brought Leila back in a way, and I couldn't get enough of my time with them. Life had settled into a comfortable rhythm that I couldn't imagine changing. If the Spirits had told me to leave now, I would have pointedly ignored them, but I hadn't heard from them in a few months. They seemed willing to just let me be, which I welcomed gladly.

It was evening, and Polly had taken the girls for their bath right after supper. I would normally have joined them, but for some reason, Mr Crowly had asked to speak privately with me. I was anxiously waiting for him in his study when he appeared. I couldn't imagine what he wanted to say since everything seemed to be going so well.

"Have I done something wrong?" I asked him as he entered, and his eyes widened with surprise. A wave of relief washed over me at this, and I relaxed a bit. I didn't think I had, but I didn't have any other ideas.

"Not at all," he assured me. "In fact, I was wondering if perhaps you'd like to talk outside instead?"

Now I was truly bewildered, but I readily agreed and followed him out onto the wide porch. Purple morning glories were starting to climb around the railings. Polly had told me by summer that the porch would be covered in them, and I couldn't wait to see.

"I cannot keep quiet any longer," Mr Crowly began earnestly, taking my hand in his. I was startled at this but didn't protest. I liked my hand in his. "You have been a blessing to this house and my life. I wanted to know if you would possibly consider staying in it forever."

"Thank you, Mr Crowly," I chuckled, shaking my head, "but the girls won't need a governess forever. They will grow up one day. Though I admit, I'll be sad to see it. I love being here with your family."

He looked bewildered and then blushed.

"You misunderstand me," he said, his words measured as he placed a light finger against my cheek. My heart stopped entirely. "Please consider staying here as my wife, not a governess."

It took a few moments to catch my breath and stop my head from spinning. Being his wife had never occurred to me, though I knew I was attracted to him. This seemed so sudden. I had only been their governess for a few months. How could he know so quickly that he wanted to marry me?

"Are you sure, Mr Crowly?" I asked, confused and wanting to clarify that I understood. "You've known me for such a short time. How can you be sure that I'm the woman fit to be your wife?"

He gave me the softest smile I had ever seen, and I felt my knees tremble.

"Because I would be honoured to have you as the mother of my children," he replied, tracing my cheek with his finger. "I have wanted you since the moment I saw you. Your beauty, wit, charm, and stubborn determination have captivated me."

His stroking finger against my cheek was nearly hypnotizing me, but not enough for me to lose my wits entirely. I stepped back, breaking our contact long enough to breathe and think rationally.

"From the moment you saw me?" I repeated, raising a brow quizzically. "Then why did you ask me to be your governess?"

He flashed me a bright smile and laughed, his humour returning.

143

"I knew I was taking you with me one way or another," he admitted, giving a rueful chuckle, "but had I proposed to you in New York, it would have been far too soon, and you'd have denied me."

I considered this, knowing he was right. It also explained why he had been so willing to buy my clothes. I stayed silent, trying to organise my thoughts and feelings. I knew the attraction between us was mutual, but I had never considered for a moment that he would be willing to take me as his wife. Knowing he wanted me filled me with such happiness that all my misgivings vanished. I had kept my feelings towards him locked tight in case they would never be returned, but now I felt free to release them.

"You're right that I would have denied you," I said finally, stepping forward to take his hand. He clenched it tightly, and my cheeks burned when I looked into his eyes and saw such intense love there. "But I won't deny you now, Mr Crowly."

"Harold, please," he whispered, pressing his forehead against mine as he finally relaxed, knowing he would never lose me.

"Harold," I said, lifting his face to look straight into his eyes. "I never thought I'd love a Yankee."

Surprised amusement lit his face, and we both laughed. He wrapped his arm around my waist and twirled me.

"You little rebel," he chuckled, kissing my cheek as we stood again. "But you're my rebel now, and I won't ever love another."

I laughed, my heart fit to explode as true contentment filled me. After all my travelling, I felt as if I had discovered the greatest treasure. Not just a place to live or a means of survival, but a family again. They could never replace the family I lost, but they filled the void I had been carrying with me. I happily imagined being the girls' mother, enjoying holidays again, and keeping a home as Mama had kept ours. As Harold bent to kiss me softly, I heard the Spirits' voice in my head.

Welcome home.

About the Author

Born in northern California, Erin specialized as an equestrian trainer in the Olympic disciplines, but her natural wanderlust led her to Ireland, where she currently resides with her husband and three children. Surrounded by the natural splendor of the emerald coast, she embraced her love for the sprawling landscape through hiking. With a particular interest in European culture and history, Erin moved into the world of literature to share her tales of journeys and adventures with fellow bookworms.

You can follow Erin on Facebook at
facebook.com/eebyrnesauthor
Learn more about Erin and other works on her
website at www.eebyrnes.com

Printed in Great Britain
by Amazon

10658106R00089